W9-BMU-910

CLAYTON COUNTY LIBRARY
865 BATTLE CREEK ROAD
JONESBORO, GA 30236

Georgia Law requires Library materials to be returned
or replacement costs paid. Failure to comply with this
law is a misdemeanor. (O.C.G.A. 20-5-53)

Uncertain

Ground

DISCARDED

Other books by Carolyn Osborn:

A Horse of Another Color

The Fields of Memory

The Grands

Warriors & Maidens

Uncertain Ground

A Novel

Carolyn Osborn

WingsPress

San Antonio, Texas
2010

Uncertain Ground © 2010 by Wings Press

Cover art: Untitled watercolor © 2009 by Barbara Whitehead

First Edition
Print Edition ISBN: 978-0-916727-67-3
ePub ISBN: 978-1-60940-009-5
Kindle ISBN: 978-1-60940-010-1
PDF ISBN: 978-1-60940-011-8

Wings Press
627 E. Guenther
San Antonio, Texas 78210
Phone/fax: (210) 271-7805

On-line catalogue and ordering:
www.wingspress.com
All Wings Press titles are distributed to the trade by
Independent Publishers Group
www.ipgbook.com

Library of Congress Cataloging-in-Publication Data:

Osborn, Carolyn, 1934-
Uncertain ground : a novel / Carolyn Osborn. -- 1st ed.
      p. cm.
   ISBN 978-0-916727-67-3 (pbk. : alk. paper) -- ISBN 978-1-60940-009-5
(epub : alk. paper) -- ISBN 978-1-60940-010-1 (kindle : alk. paper) --
ISBN 978-1-60940-011-8 (library pdf : alk. paper)
1. Self-realization in women--Fiction. 2. Galveston Island (Tex.)--Fiction.
3. Texas--History--20th century--Fiction. I. Title.
   PS3565.S348U53 2010
   813'.54--dc22
                        2010004352

Except for fair use in reviews and/or scholarly considerations,
no portion of this book may be reproduced in any form without the written permission of the author or the publisher.

*For Joe Osborn
and Edward Simmen, B.O.I.*

Uncertain Ground

Observe always that everything is the result of a change, and get used to thinking that there is nothing Nature loves so. . . .
        —Marcus Aurelius, *Meditations*

The nature of the soil on which Galveston is built (is) a mixture of mud and sand generally up to the ankles of the pedestrian.
        —*The Journal of Francis Sheridan,* 1839

When I first saw the Mclean house again I wanted to run up the steps and bang on the front door with both fists. Being thrown forward to the present by simply turning a corner was such a shock my first impulse was anger. I'd driven there early in the morning, had set aside the time to go and see the house I'd known, so I was already seeing it in my mind, a classic late Victorian island house, narrow, its boards glistening white, two story with dark green shutters, a black wrought iron fence on two sides, and high gray painted steps leading to a small front porch with a shiny white paneled door, an entrance repeated on the west side where there was a smaller landing. Beside the west porch a large palm tree rose.

But when I drove by the west side and around the corner, I found nothing but a wreck, a hodgepodge of apartments, each with its own entrance, one in front, one on the side, probably more in back. The fence had disappeared, the high gray steps had been replaced by raw boards and unpainted railings, the green shutters were now a nasty, peeling mustard yellow, a few shingles—edged by worn gray—hung on by single nails. The palm tree, at least, still stood on the west side. The house, so marked by make-do, so changed by junky renovations, was so obviously full of other lives that I wanted to protest, to beat on the grimy front door, and at the same moment I also wanted to summon everyone I knew who'd lived there the summer of fifty-three—Bertha, Mowrey, Emmett, and the one who visited most, Luis—as if the five of us might recapture that time.

Chapter One

Emmett nearly missed the train to Galveston because he'd walked down to the corral to see a new quarter horse that had been delivered to Uncle Estes early that morning. Aunt Earlene was fuming when they finally arrived. She and Emmett had driven from the ranch near Mullin, a little bit of a town thirty miles south of Leon where we lived.

"Martha, why your brother had to have that horse sent to him this morning, and why Emmett had to go down to see it, I'll never know!" She complained to my mother while Emmett stalked off away from us to a far corner of the platform to search for the train.

Mother smiled, "Well you know Estes and horses."

She couldn't bring herself to blame her youngest brother for anything, nor could she blame his son either. It wasn't that they could do no wrong. She simply found it impossible to call them to account for whatever they did. Earlene, on the other hand, found Estes and Emmett far short of her expectations frequently. She had the look of a scold—a long face, a prominent nose, snapping dark eyes, dark hair drawn into a knot on the back of her head. Her reactions were generally exaggerated, and she was aware they were. She tried to restrain frown wrinkles by clamping her mouth shut and stretching her forehead into bland smoothness. It never worked. Whenever she attempted a placid look, she seemed about to explode from impatience.

My mother was more like her brother Estes, even-tempered, not easily angered though she could be aroused. No matter how kind she was, a special tension existed between her and Earlene, partially based on their feelings about Estes, I supposed. No matter how hard she tried, she found Earlene difficult. It wasn't Mother's fault that some people were more loveable than others although she often felt it was.

As for Estes and Earlene's son, he was another matter. Mother simply acknowledged Emmett, accepted him as she accepted her brother. Earlene, on the other hand, didn't want her son to be like his father.

I couldn't see anything particularly wrong with Uncle Estes. He was as even-tempered as Mother and as obliging. There was a sort of sweetness about him and ease, for he tended to smile broadly as if continually affirming he found you as intelligent and agreeable as he was. And he waited to hear what other people had to say. Emmett, I understood then, was to have all his father's virtues and more, but what else did Aunt Earlene think was necessary?

"Polish," my mother told me, "and education. Estes only went to college two years. Earlene didn't finish either, and she still thinks she should have."

Emmett quit prowling the west end of the platform to join us. It was nearly ten in the morning, already hot of course. Sun beat down on the red brick depot, and intense heat rose from already over-baked earth marking another long day of drought. We waited outside in the deep shade of the porch's high arches. Aunt Earlene and Emmett had been up since five, at least, since they were meeting us at the nearest Santa Fe station, about twenty miles south of Leon in Temple. Getting out of the middle of Texas required way too much time, I thought. Emmett was used to driving for miles to get anywhere, but he wasn't in a good humor that morning; neither was I, but I was hiding my dismal mood. I even took a certain pride in not letting anyone know how I was feeling. Emmett's display was enough.

"I told you we had plenty of time, Mama. I haven't even heard a train yet, much less seen one. I bet it's three counties west of here still, and there you are standing out in the heat."

"Emmett, I don't care if it's four counties away. We can catch the Santa Fe here only on Mondays and Thursdays. I'd rather be a little early than miss it, wouldn't you?"

He stomped toward the end of the platform again; since he had on his boots, we could hear him easily. He was also wearing a pair of twill pants and a white shirt that Earlene must have made him put on. Left to himself he'd never wear anything but boots, jeans, and the nearest plaid shirt. At least that's all I usually saw him in.

"He can't stand being crossed about anything," Earlene commented. "He'd rather miss a train than be wrong."

So had she, not that I would tell her. Aunt Earlene was a force, one to be contradicted or evaded. If you voiced disagreement, you were in for a long fight. Emmett had decided it wasn't worth it that morning. I kept my mouth shut while Emmett kept his distance.

Mother tried distracting her by mentioning the sales in Waco. They were both great shoppers. Though they preferred the Dallas stores, Waco was a lot nearer and not to be overlooked.

In five minutes more, the train had pulled up, heat shimmering in waves against its silvery cars. A porter helped me on while Earlene hollered for Emmett who'd circled back from the platform and disappeared inside the station.

He ambled out as if he were going nowhere in particular, as if there wasn't a train in front of him, stooped to allow his mother to kiss his cheek, and letting his suitcase bump his leg, climbed in the passenger car. Once on board, he settled next to me on the scratchy seat in his usual slouch. I got up and went across the aisle to wave goodbye to Mother and Earlene.

As we pulled away from the station, I turned back to Emmett. "You're not happy about this trip I see."

"Celia, don't you know I'm being sent?"

"You'd rather stay in the middle of Texas in August when you could be down at the coast?" Escaping summer heat, if only for a little while, was considered a necessity in my family.

"Yeah." He turned toward the window to look at the outskirts as we moved out of town. I couldn't find much of interest, but Emmett maintained it looked different from the train.

He had dark hair like his mother, olive-skin like Estes and Mother. Beyond that he was himself, good looking, I supposed, if a little sullen at the moment. He had deep brown eyes and wide set lips that could widen into a smile as generous as his father's. It was odd to be sitting next to him. Unless it was a ceremonial occasion such as Thanksgiving or Christmas, I generally saw him outside on horseback riding off with my brother, Kenyon, or leaning against a corral fence behind his house at the ranch. He lived way out in the country west of Mullin, went to a different high school and a different college; mine was UT while his was A&M. I saw him infrequently and, except for family gatherings, mainly as a lanky, restless figure in the landscape. When he came inside he grew awkward and uncomfortable. He bumped into tables, knocked against door frames, sometimes leaned against pictures on the wall, and continually nudged floor lamps and coffee tables until someone, usually his mother, reminded him he needed to avoid them. No matter where he was in a house, there wasn't quite enough room for him.

Even though we were both twenty Emmett seemed younger, in part because he was generally in trouble just as my brother Kenyon was, and in part because he'd never left Texas except for brief forays across the border from Laredo to Nueva Laredo. Despite settling in Leon, I 'd seen a wider world. Like most army brats, I'd lived in a different places—in Tennessee, Florida, and Texas—and I'd gone away to summer schools in Colorado and Mexico.

To me, Emmett was so rooted in one place he couldn't find his way out, nor did he particularly want to be anywhere else. I grew restless when I had to stay in Leon long. There wasn't enough there, not enough to do, not even enough to look at. In search of distraction I read a lot and sometimes picked up *Life* magazine. As if waiting for me, I found among the coverage of national news, a report on the Texas drought with full-page pictures of dead cattle laying on bare soil. The train was carrying us through that same kind of pasture land now mixed at times with fields of oats, corn, and maize, all shriveled to dust-colored tan, all stunted by the long drought. I opened the book I'd brought with me.

Turning back toward me from the window, he asked, "You know why Mama wanted me to go to Galveston so much, don't you?"

I put the book aside. "I can guess."

"Yeah. Doris."

"Again?"

"Again."

Both of us knew he'd already been required to spend the month of June in the country near Laredo. He'd had a great time working at Uncle Blanton's ranch all week and making the bars on the weekends. Although he had no gift for languages, he swore his Spanish had improved. Emmett's version of Spanish was a sort of pidgin make-do. "You savvy?" he would ask, and I'd always think of corny cowboys wearing white hats in western serials I'd seen on Saturday afternoons when I was younger. If I corrected him, I'd only be corrected in turn for speaking school Spanish. It was an old and fruitless argument for the truth was, as my father had pointed out, Emmett didn't believe he'd ever need anything but bad Spanish, an assumption my father laughed about while I could see nothing but arrogance. His fight with his mother over Doris Lacey was different.

She was, in Earlene's eyes, a sexual threat, the country high school beauty who might lure Emmett into marriage too young, the appealing daughter of a dirt farmer who, in Earlene's eyes, was only angling for a part of the largest ranch in the area. Emmett, his mother believed, was meant for a better match, so he was being shipped off for the second time that summer before he got Doris pregnant. None of this hysteria had been discussed openly in the family. My father had said, "Emmett could get that girl in trouble," and meant it. But no one ever said the question of Emmett's marriage was the key part of his mother's plan for his future social standing.

Instead they insisted Uncle Estes wanted to keep him away from rodeos. Though no one in the family had seen him do it, Emmett had been riding saddle broncs in the smaller rodeos around Mullin. Estes, I guessed, probably really didn't mind much. He'd grown up on a ranch, had broken his share of horses.

"Are they sending you away from somebody?" Emmett asked.

"Not exactly." It was true I'd been unhappy ever since I got home from summer school in Colorado, and my parents had probably guessed it had to do with Tony Gregory. I'd told them little about him except his name and the fact I'd spent most of my free time with him. Staying there for the second six weeks proved to be an impossibility since I'd promised to be a bridesmaid in a friend's July wedding in Leon. Flying back and forth to Boulder was a frivolity my parents wouldn't pay for, especially since they had also guessed correctly that I was more interested in Tony than I was in school. After the wedding there were few distractions in Leon. Two of my other high school friends had married and left. The rest, like me, helped their mothers at home and met in the late afternoons at the municipal swimming pool. Early one morning I tried riding horseback with a friend, but the road was so dusty and the country so dry, we were home in two hours. On weekends we dated whoever was in town, no one much.

Could anyone have believed a trip would cure me of longing, that a change of scene would make that much difference? I doubted it though I knew my parents held onto some old saws, and what if they did? Nearly anything would be better than finishing the summer in Leon.

"I don't mind going. I haven't been down there in years. I like the beach, don't you?"

"No."

"What do you plan to do then?"

"Celia, I don't plan. Come on. Let's go find out if this train has a diner. I'm hungry."

It was early, only eleven-thirty, but I got up and swayed down the aisle after him, rocked with the train though all the dusty brown country, traveling as fast as it could take us toward the sea. I guessed Mother and my aunt had decided I could look after Emmett, an idea I didn't relish. My own life was so confused I'd been dreaming of the lulling calm of days sitting on the beach staring at the Gulf. Now it appeared that dream might evaporate. At a distance I got along with Emmett well enough. I even liked what I knew of Doris Lacey though she, too, was someone I didn't know well. She was just finishing high school in Mullin. Like so many boys from small towns and large who went away to college, Emmett kept his serious girl friend at home. She was the one he saw the first night he came back and the last night before he left. I'd seen her in Leon at the movies with him once or twice. She didn't cling, didn't hang onto him as if she wanted to own him, nor did she seem to agree with him about everything. Doris had a toughness I admired, envied in a way. During rodeos she entered the barrel races, and they required superior riding. I wasn't interested in riding figure eights around three barrels in a row, however I'd ridden enough horses to respect her skill. I'd only seen her race once. She did it the usual way, leaning almost out of the saddle on the turns, her right arm raised high as she whipped the horse's flank on the last one. But hers was the best-trained horse—she wheeled him so close to the barrels they were almost touching—and the fastest that night.

"Do you really mind going?" I asked Emmett when we'd taken seats in the diner.

"No. Doris will be there when I get back. The funny thing is, Cousin, we're on our way to Sin City."

I laughed. He sounded so much like he'd just finished a long trail drive and was looking forward to liberty. Post Office Street in Galveston was well known as the biggest red light district in Texas. There you could buy mixed drinks across the bar when people in the rest of the state were carrying their whisky bottles around in obvious brown paper sacks and joining spurious private clubs in order to drink cocktails away from home. Gambling was another public pleasure. The whole state had evidently agreed that Galveston could be the one open city.

"They've got slot machines everywhere, and I've already got plenty of change," said Emmett. He raised his glass of water. "Here's to a fine time!"

I raised a glass to meet his but as I drank from it I could barely pretend to agree. It seemed entirely unlikely that I'd stand much of a chance of steering Emmett away from Post Office Street, bars, and slot machines. On the other hand, I didn't want to believe I was altogether responsible for him since Emmett was, I felt, already beyond anyone's control.

After lunch we spread out. Emmett was so big he could easily take up two seats. The Santa Fe carried wheat from Kansas, cotton from the high plains, and sulfur from towns on down the line, but only a few passengers that day. No one raised cotton around Leon or Temple any more, and not many people seemed to be on their way to the Gulf just then. Across the aisle from Emmett I watched him fall asleep calmed by the rhythm of the wheels clacking. I remained awake envying him his ease even if he was snoring. I'd taken the train back to Tennessee to visit my father's relatives often in the summers. A book could usually overcome repetitious landscape, so I read my way through northeast Texas and most of Arkansas each time. Now I was headed southeast, and my accumulated worries, including how Emmett and I would get along, could be suspended by someone else's story. But I let the book slide. The first time I went to Galveston kept coming to mind.

We'd almost floated in. The moment we crossed the causeway linking the island to the mainland and hit Broadway, water began rising in the car floor. Dumped by a storm that had just passed over the island, water rocked around the floorboard. Kenyon and I sat together on the back seat, both of us scared, our feet tucked beneath us. He poked me in the ribs as the water sloshed against the car's doors. I poked him back. Neither one of us said a word, nor did our father. But he would. I could feel his temper rising like the water. Our mother smiled at us over the back of the seat.

"I thought you said there was a sea-wall here, Martha." Our father's voice, though terse, was clearly accusing.

"Don't worry," she said. "Galveston floods so easy. It'll go down in a little while."

I looked out the window to an old cemetery where graves, sheathed in stone, had been raised above ground. Gray water lapped against their marble sides so they seemed to rock like awkward boats in an uneasy harbor. All the world was asway. I nudged Kenyon who made an awful face by opening his mouth, turning his lips down on both sides, and widening his eyes. His pantomime terror mirrored our fears and mocked them. The graves, I noticed, sat higher than we did.

"I didn't know it was going to rain. Did you, Will?" Our mother's voice was patient yet firm. He could blame her if he pleased, but the weather was not her fault. After all the seawall was for seawater. This was plain old rain.

I could remember only a little about that first trip. The rain did stop before we got to the Mcleans' house. Sun broke through while we were still driving down Broadway where the center strip was covered with pink oleanders, glistening with water. We turned the corner by a white towered multidomed Catholic Church that looked, I first thought, like something out of the *Arabian Nights*. Once we were off the boulevard the rain subsided. Down the street a few blocks from the church was the Mclean house.

Dazzling white, two-story frame—the shingles were added later—its long green shutters covered the downstairs windows keeping the interior dark and cool, protecting those who lived there and keeping their secrets. One tall palm, that postcard emblem of sunny tropical places, stood on the corner. Sitting on top of low brick piers, the house was supported also by ships' timbers, the concealed reminder of its builder, Mowrey Mclean's father, a Scottish sea captain. It had weathered high winds, floods, hurricanes and the 1900 storm.

There was a one-story frame house in need of a coat of paint next door; it was so covered by oleanders that the need wasn't too evident. Across the street another much larger house with a set of four columns, also surrounded by shrubbery and palms, showed its weather worn boards more obviously. That was the way Galveston neighborhoods in the older part of town looked, a surface mixture of rich and poor, but just as often, I supposed, of enterprise and negligence, of diligence and procrastination. People could be careless about paint in Galveston, partially because salt air attacked everything indiscriminately, partially because individuality was understood in this seaport city in some way it wasn't in a small town.

The first visit was brief, only a weekend. What I kept of it mainly was memories of the rain, the house, a few parts of its interior and the novelty of walking five blocks to the beach with Kenyon, Mother, and my aunt Bertha—fat, cheerful, middle-aged, her olive skin already quite wrinkled, not pretty but lively. Five years older than Mother, her good humor matched her inclination toward bossiness. Both she and Mother were wearing old saggy bathing suits, which they laughed about saying they belonged to "the rough stone ages." They had both bought their suits years before the war began. That was the way everyone divided time then, before and after the war and no one asked which war.

We made that trip almost a year after we'd moved to Texas. Now, seven years later I was twenty, getting ready to begin my sophomore year in college. For a month I would be living with two people I didn't really know. As for Emmett, I barely knew him either. Well, I'd become accustomed to living with strangers before. At school I'd had to get to know roommates, and of course, I wouldn't be rooming with Emmett.

Since late afternoon, we'd been staring out at the flat green coastal plain, surrounding the tracks. Now and then we saw white egrets balanced on cattle backs or a lone heron fishing. Even before the train crossed the railroad bridge over the bay, before smelling salt air and glimpsing the undersides of gulls flying, before the porter came through our car almost singing Gal-ves-ton, I pictured the Mclean house waiting for us.

Chapter Two

Two days after we arrived, after I'd spent half a morning strolling around the neighborhood and an hour writing a long letter to Tony Gregory, I wandered into the living room of the Mclean house where no one ever seemed to go. On the dining room wall behind me were two separately framed birds' nests where stuffed bluebirds hovered over tiny powdery white eggs in nests, one bird and three eggs per nest, a strange precision. Why would anyone want to arrest that particular moment under glass twice? There was nothing like those birds in any of the other family houses. My Grandmother Henderson's living room in Nashville almost rattled with carved walnut leaves. There were some sort of birds' talons on her bathtubs, but there were no stuffed birds. As far as I could tell, useless things appealed to Bertha. Out in the hall a hat rack and umbrella stand held five hats nobody wore, and although I'd been told it rained often in the afternoons, there were no umbrellas.

In the living room marble-topped tables and fat globular oil lamps, now converted to electricity, crowded the spaces between chairs, couch, and rectangular patches of oriental rugs. Against one wall stood a secretary with top shelves full of narrow leather-bound books behind glass. The spines were upright, their gilt letters unblemished; apparently neither Aunt Bertha nor Uncle Mowrey nor any of the Mcleans preceding them had ever touched a one. They were there obviously because they fit the shelves. The titles were familiar; *The Poetry of Robert Burns*, *Three Plays*, Wm. Shakespeare, *The Lady of the Lake*, Scott, the same kind of well respected unread books that everybody in their generation seemed to have. A figure of a dog of mystifying breed, something that could have been an ashtray shaped like a pair of hands with empty white palms uplifted, roses made of paper and cotton somewhere in Mexico, and a cut-glass bowl of terribly fake red cherries were scattered about the room.

All these things seemed to have particular places as if permanence might bring order to the whole assortment. I looked down at three tightly draped buxom ladies who supported a marble table top on their heads and laughed. The ladies were, at least, useful. Like my Tennessee grandmother, the Mcleans accumulated things and apparently never rid themselves of any object they ever owned no matter whether they had bought or inherited it.

I jumped when Aunt Bertha stuck her head in the doorway, the rest of her almost disembodied in the dark hall.

"What are you doing in there?"

It wasn't an unfriendly question; she was simply curious.

"Just looking. You've got a lot of antiques."

"Mostly Mother Mclean's passed down to Mowrey with the house. You like antiques?"

I didn't. I longed for the spare lines of modern Scandinavian design, for light, not for rooms darkened to save Victorian furniture's patina and the oriental rugs' colors. I wanted open, uncurtained windows I could see the world through.

"Mother does." I said.

"But you?"

"Some. I'm used to them."

She didn't press further. "I'm going upstairs for a nap. Summer afternoons make me drowsy."

I'd been surprised by her cheerful reference to Mother Mclean. Mother thought of her otherwise. "Mean . . . penny pinching. She wouldn't pay for a maid when she could have well afforded to, and she kept Bertha working in that house like she was a slave." Once free of her mother-in-law, Bertha didn't seem to mind keeping her furniture. Perhaps she'd looked after the household so long everything seemed like her own by the time the old lady died.

I eyed the copper colored chandelier with its daffodil shaped shades reflected in a long gilt-framed mirror that faintly distorted images. Wary of seeing myself pulled out of shape in the darkened room, I kept away from the mirror. It wasn't like a fun house mirror, although I didn't like the way they turned people into freaks either. Aunt Bertha's mirror pushed eyes further up into foreheads, elongated noses. Remembering my first visit's reflection, I knew it would nudge familiar features vaguely askew and this was more threatening than a fun house mirror; it merely hinted at the grotesque and provoked fear of what else might be lurking. Dreading that possibility, I began to search for something more reassuring.

Since we'd lived in Nashville near relatives, their things had become so familiar I'd almost stopped seeing them, but the houses of my Texas kin held sets of clues, suggestions about unknown people with unknown characteristics. Aunt Earlene, I'd noticed seemed to revere Jensen silver, or anything else she might buy at Neiman-Marcus. Like Mother and Aunt Bertha, she prized antiques. Uncle Estes who had little interest in objects other than guns and saddles, did like old straight chairs with cowhide seats. He was permitted to keep one in the kitchen.

Keeping my back to Bertha's mirror, I picked up a book of pictures of French cathedrals. There was the angel I liked, the smiling angel of Rheims, holding stone robes so lightly that they seemed made of silk, making a joyful proclamation: Catholicism is the true religion. I'd given the book to Aunt Bertha and Uncle Mowrey for Christmas. Had they ever done anything more than idly turn pages as I was doing? For most of Mother's family, newspapers were enough. She and Earlene read house magazines, the big glossy ones with pictures of totally clean, totally unobtainable rooms where everything matched beautifully or clashed stylishly, a perfection neither one of them really hoped to achieve. Perhaps they just liked knowing such rooms existed somewhere. Estes thumbed through *Time* occasionally. None of them read like my father, Kenyon, and I. All of us lived with our noses in books. My father swore he couldn't go to sleep without reading something first. Next to us, Bertha hardly read at all. That was one reason I'd chosen a picture book—that and the

Catholicism. The Chandlers were Methodists except for Bertha who'd become a Catholic when she married.

"Scotch Catholics, all the Mcleans were," Mother said. "Mama nearly died when they married."

I knew about religious conflicts in the South. I hadn't thought they had moved to Texas. According to Mother when she was a girl, Granny Chandler hadn't approved of drinking, dancing, card playing, and Catholicism. I felt she had a weak sense of sin. What about killing and rape and dropping atom bombs?

Granny must have given up on Mother since she and my father drank at home, in other people's houses, at the Ft. Hood's Officer's Club where they also danced. Card playing was definitely acceptable. Women met with others at bridge clubs all over town. As for Catholicism, in Leon it was generally left to a few Anglos and the Mexican population. A small group of them clustered around an equally small church on the east highway near the outskirts of town.

I had never gone inside that church. I doubted anybody else I knew had either.

Granny Chandler, a pleasant, round-faced lady in her seventies, stayed in Mullin safely removed from the wickedness of Galveston or Leon. She'd been a frontier sort of woman, one who lived in a place not really ready for settlement till after the Civil War. The Comanches had roamed freely around there, a fact Emmett told me with great pleasure. He was so dark-skinned he might have been part Indian himself.

Though Granny had forbidden Aunt Bertha to join the church, the rest of the family, both her brothers and her sister, seemed to ignore the Mcleans' religion. Amazed at the strength of old prejudices, I remained curious. I could, I suppose, ask her how she felt about becoming a Catholic; however, I was too unsure about how she'd react, and I would never have waked up anybody to ask such a question. She was napping by now beneath a dried palm cross tacked on the wall above her head-board. Even if she were given to abrupt questions herself, she'd be too upset over losing her nap to give a clear answer. I could imagine her rising up hollering, sitting straight up in bed, a plump middle-aged woman multiplied nine times by triple mirrors on each of the three dressers stationed around the room. Across from her bedstead was Uncle Mowrey's.

She slept happily surrounded by her nest of dressers, a chair, and a small daybed. Too small for me or for Emmett— unused except as a catchall for Bertha's treasures—the daybed was covered with bits of frayed tapestry that might become pillow covers if she ever got around to making them, boxes of last year's Christmas decorations, a clutter of costume jewelry, and an amber rosary that had been blessed by the pope.

"It got broken anyway," Bertha sighed, then laughed.

The day we arrived, she led us to our part of the bedroom, a double-sized space since the sliding doors which would have ordinarily made two bedrooms had been pushed wide open.

I saw then that she meant for Emmett and me to sleep on the twin beds straight across from hers and Uncle Mowrey's.

"We all need the draft." Bertha pointed to the tall front and back windows, the only one without curtains in the house.

"You want us both here?" I was so surprised I asked out loud. I'd expected a room of my own. Why couldn't Emmett have slept on the couch downstairs? That was the way Kenyon and I had slept when we first visited. Now Emmett had to have the only other bed in the house, one next to mine separated by a narrow strip of rug and Bertha's supposed supervision. Uncle Mowrey, slightly deaf already, wouldn't have heard an approaching bomb, and he was, I thought, generally so unnoticing he wouldn't see somebody tap dancing naked in front of him.

"Well, Celia, after all, you are cousins." She smiled as if she had said the most ordinary thing.

Emmett grinned, hung a few things in the closet, and dumped this suitcase under the bed. He'd been living out of it mostly ever since. I'd emptied mine into one of the dressers and the closet. I wanted to slam the door when I finished, but Aunt Bertha was waiting on her side of the room so I didn't. I was still unhappy in that bedroom with Emmett. I had to make sure he wasn't around or go to the bathroom to dress and undress. And when I walked out, I had to make sure I had enough clothes on. At home I could wander around in a slip or pajamas. Not here. At the first sight of my blue-flower-sprigged shortie pajamas Emmett had given me a mock leer, just enough of one to let me know he was watching. When I added a robe, he stood by his bed wearing only a pair of drawstring pajama bottoms and laughed. Despising being made to feel too prim, I pulled the robe off and got the leer once more. When I got into bed, I turned my back on him. A flush broke over my neck and down my shoulders as if I were standing under a warm shower. I rolled over and threw my pillow at him. He wouldn't give it back.

"I'll have to ask Aunt Bertha for another one," I whispered.

He laughed and tossed it toward me as if he'd planned to all along, and for that moment, I wasn't an equal. I was only about ten-years-old and at the mercy of a slightly indulgent, much older boy.

I needed a place to be by myself, a room with a door I could shut. Kenyon and I had shared a bedroom until I was six. Since then, except for the semesters away, I'd had a room of my own. Emmett and Uncle Mowrey both snored. So did Aunt Bertha sometimes. So did I maybe. I didn't know. My roommates at the university hadn't complained so far.

We'd only been in Galveston two days. The first I spent mainly at the beach only four or five blocks away. I hadn't minded being there alone with the low waves, the gray-brown sand, the huge light blue sky that turned almost white at noon. So much of my life I'd spent visiting old people's houses—especially Grandmother Henderson's in Tennessee during the war—waiting for time to pass, waiting for my father to come home, waiting to grow up. Granny Chandler's in Mullin was the one we often visited on Sundays now. It smelled different, not of soot, old wood, lemon oil, and medicine I remembered. Granny Chandler's smelled of gas fires and a whiff of decay I associated with talcum powder and earth. I wanted to escape all those smells, the darkness of those old houses, to be outside, to be alone.

It had been hot on Galveston beach yesterday, hotter than many summer days I'd known, but the sea was fresh and clear, the tides so slight when I was there that, despite the long slow slope of the continental shelf, the water had hardly roiled the sand. Other days near the shore the little waves would be light brown. I'd seen it that way before. Yesterday the Gulf had been perfect, and lying on a big towel on the blistering sand, wearing over my bathing suit a soft old cotton shirt that Mother had insisted I bring, I'd slept for a few moments in silent animal comfort, undistracted by anyone, hearing only distant voices of children playing and the quiet shush-shush of waves drowning traffic noise on the seawall above. Once I heard gulls cry, but that was all. My legs, unprotected by the shirt, were slightly burned. I'd keep off the beach today. Late in the afternoon I might walk back over to the boulevard to see if I could hear the man playing. He wasn't exactly black but deep brown, the color of strong tea. Yesterday he'd stationed himself on the steps of one of the piers, the one where all the giant conch shells were sold. Next to him was a barrel painted in wild zigzags, yellow, red, black, and white.

"A drum, isn't it?"

"Yeah. I play most times in the night. You never hear me before?"

I shook my head.

"You come here this night or the next. I be here then." He was speaking with an accent I'd never heard.

"Where are you from?"

"Another island, child, in another sea."

"Which one?"

"Jamaica. Far out in the ocean." He exaggerated o-ce-an making it sound as wavy as water.

I tried to imagine it then, another island far out in the ocean, but I couldn't remember where oceans stopped and seas began on any map. Who decided that kind of thing anyway?

Who drew those invisible lines? Aunt Bertha had an old atlas somewhere. I could at least look up Jamaica. After all I was a journalism student, uncertain as to whether I'd stick with it, but already trained to make sure of locations.

Remembering I hadn't looked for Jamaica yet, I stared toward the little alcove dividing the dining room from the kitchen, a place where things and people seemed to collect. I thought I'd seen that atlas bulging out of a shelf back there.

On my way through the room, the phone rang. I hoped it wasn't Emmett in trouble already. He hadn't wanted to go to the beach yesterday, and I didn't know where he'd gone that morning.

"Celia, get in the car and come on down here and get me."

"I can't get you unless I know where you are."

The receiver on the other end fell with a clunk against a wall or the floor somewhere. I could barely hear a country-western wail over the murmur of people talking. A motor started and sighed dead then started again. I sat down on the floor wondering if somebody had to go and get him all the time when he was exiled to Laredo. Probably not since he was with Alex, Uncle Blanton's son. Blanton lived in town with his wife Ellen, Alex who was Emmett's age, and a daughter, Marie. Evidently Emmett was kept busy all week at the ranch then turned loose with Alex to roam on the weekends. There were no rodeos nearby, but there were plenty of bars and boys' town in Nuevo Laredo, with its shanties full of prostitutes, was more interesting—he'd let me know—than any particular girl.

"I'm at West Beach."

"How far down?"

"Damned if I know." He laughed.

I was sure he was drunk then. When he drank he had a half crazy kind of laugh, a low chuckle that reached higher and higher. I'd heard it before in a honky-tonk cafe near McGregor, the first wet town across the line from Leon where everybody came from all the dry counties around to drink beer. I cringed inwardly when I heard Emmett's whoop across the room.

Getting drunk was all right; showing it wasn't. He didn't seem to know it that night in McGregor and he hadn't learned it yet. Still waiting on him, I watched the slits of sunlight poke through the dark shutters on the west side and fall across the carpet's mass of faded blue flowers to my feet.

He coughed into the phone.

"Don't do that."

"Always saying 'don't'."

"Wonder what the name of that place is?" I spoke slower than usual, trying not to show concern.

"No name . . . no name atall. This is the No-Name Bar."

He seemed to be losing interest in going anywhere.

"I'm in this no-name place and I like it." He was almost singing.

"What does the outside look like?"

"Great big red sign says beer."

"And what else?'

"Flags . . . little bitty pieces of things blowing."

"You mean pennants? You be out front, okay?" I didn't want to have to go inside and try to drag him out.

"Celia?"

"Yes?" The phone fell again.

From a little distance, as if he'd fallen on the floor and the receiver was dangling beside him, I heard him laughing. Useless as it was, I wanted to shout at him.

"Celia? You still there?"

"No. I'm somewhere else."

"Bring a beer when you come. Better bring two." He hung up abruptly.

Probably they wouldn't sell him anymore. There was usually some beer in Aunt Bertha's refrigerator. I found two cans and put them in a sack telling myself it was part of the placating a drunk routine, then I turned on the gas under a pot of water on the stove. As soon as it boiled, I threw in a couple of teaspoonfuls of instant coffee that would taste terrible. Somewhere amidst the clutter of Bertha's shelves I found a thermos. It was better, I decided, to keep the daytime drinking secret. I knew the Chandlers already had one alcoholic—Uncle Blanton's visits to Leon were infrequent mainly because he drank too much to suit my mother—and I'd noticed the whole family was on the lookout for another. It was as if they had decided one had to turn up in every generation.

In my parents' house, in Earlene and Estes's, and at the Mcleans,' the rule was no drinking before five in the afternoon. Anybody who had to have a drink before then was in real danger. Rules wouldn't keep Emmett sober. Rules were only temptations to him. Yesterday he'd managed to lose a hundred dollars playing slot machines, he'd already told me.

I closed the kitchen door behind me carefully, caught the screen so only a single low ting could be heard and walked across the back porch through the yard, through a tropical world of deep shade, pink, red and yellow hibiscus, magenta and white oleanders, their lush fragrance mixed with smells of mold, rotting wood and iodine tinged salt spray. My feet crunched the crumbled gray and white oyster shells strewn on paths and used for sidewalks all over Galveston. Behind me was an old oak water cistern, there since the sea captain's time, and still used to catch rainwater; behind it the house rose on its stubby brick-covered piers. On the second story Bertha still slept. I'd left her a note on the kitchen table.

By the gate I picked a red hibiscus and stuck it over one ear. I'd cut my hair so short that the stem of the flower poked through it reminding me of the picture of the Balinese woman on the over-sized menu Bertha had shown me yesterday. The Balinese Room, way out on a private pier, showed its guests a portrait of a brown-skinned woman with a red flower tucked behind one ear; her glossy black hair fell in a luxuriant wave around the flower. The image, especially the flat planes of the woman's face, must have been taken from something by Gauguin. With my short blonde hair, blue eyes, rounded cheeks and a slightly burned over summer tan on my legs, I looked nothing like that ideal South Sea Islander. Aunt Bertha meant to take us to the Balinese Room. She had a lot of plans for us, she said, as soon we got our sea legs. Emmett hadn't understood her. Most of the time he didn't listen well when his mother or his aunts were talking.

"She wants us just to sit around here?" He asked.

"She just thinks we need to get used to the island. Old people always talk like that. Don't you know? They think it takes time to adjust."

"I'm already used to this place," he insisted.

"I can't help that."

Out on the pavement, heat struck. My first impulse was to turn and run toward the steamy shade of the backyard again. We had a morning and an evening breeze, but in the afternoons all the winds blowing over Texas seemed to die there before the oncoming sea. Once the sun hit my head at the same time heat rose from the asphalt, a siesta seemed the best, actually the only sensible way, to endure a Galveston summer.

Emmett had left Bertha's car parked in the sun. He hadn't thought to find a tree to put it under. I reached for the keys under the seat. He didn't believe someone else might look there, and if I hadn't insisted on him hiding them, he would have left keys dangling in the ignition. Emmett had never had anything stolen from him in his life. He could walk off and leave a horse ground-tied and expect to find it waiting for him for hours. I kept telling him he wasn't in Mullin.

Circling the block, all the windows down, I headed for the seawall. It would be cooler there despite the glare. By the time I found Emmett the afternoon would be almost gone. With one hand on the steering wheel, I lit a cigarette. I still didn't smoke in front of my parents. Although my father smoked, he didn't approve of me doing it. Mother had escaped the habit after trying it. Emmett smoked too, which didn't keep him from telling me not to stick cigarettes in one corner of my mouth.

"It makes you look tough."

"So what."

"It makes you look like a whore."

Except for fighting over the pillow, that was the only argument we'd had so far on this trip. I didn't think it would be the last one. Though I had a bunch of second cousins in Tennessee on my father's side, I had only one other first cousin, Gene Walker. We never argued. He was too much older and had gone off to prep school then to Yale to study architecture. I doubted Emmett could even imagine someone like him. The idea of them meeting made me laugh out loud.

A breeze pushed smoke in my eyes. I threw the cigarette out in front of the Amusement Pier. Emmett wouldn't go out there. He thought it looked too healthy. "A nice, clean place for the kiddies to go for good, clean fun," he'd said, nor was he interested in going to the movies. He'd only have to see them again when they finally arrived in Leon, he said.

Mainly it seemed he was going to go to joints and get drunk or to other joints where he would play slot machines, lose, and then get drunk. I didn't want to spend the whole month going after him. We might be cousins, but he didn't feel like one.

The road slanted down from the seawall to the beach turning from cement to hard-packed sand. Before he was born, before cars had been invented, Uncle Mowrey told me, stagecoach drivers had used the beach to carry passengers and mail from Galveston west to San Luis Pass. A coach boarded two ferries during the trip, one to San Luis, another at the mainland where it traveled south to Matagordo. There were no ferries there now. Galveston Island's western tip ran out toward San Luis pass and that was the end of it. The westward mainland towns on the other side of the pass still existed. San Luis was gone, he said. Mowrey was a patient teller, an easy one. He knew I wouldn't know the names of any of those places, so he added compass points, giving me a notion of how to chart my way across his well-known world.

"Tell about Jean Laffite," Emmett interrupted. "And the red house. That's what he called it, the house he built here and painted red all over. Old Jean Laffite." He shook his head in silent admiration as if he would have happily joined Laffite's band of pirates.

"Are you going on another hunt?" Uncle Mowrey turned to me. "When Emmett was eight or nine . . . another time when he was down here, Bertha kept him busy digging for Lafitte's treasure in the backyard." He smiled.

Chagrined by this memory, Emmett wandered off leaving me to talk to Uncle Mowrey who wasn't in a talking mood often. I asked him what had happened to San Luis.

"Washed away. I don't know which storm. It usually takes more than one to wash a place out. People are stubborn. They keep trying to hold on. It was like that here after the 1900 storm. This house rode it out, but most of the rest of Galveston was a pile of boards after. We built it back. I was five then and I still remember that storm. Everybody who was here does."

I wanted him to tell me more about it, but he wouldn't. He was ready to take his evening walk.

Driving west along the end of the boulevard and down the ramp to the beach I tried to imagine it without umbrellas and pop bottles and people in bathing suits, tried to see it with nothing but sea and sand, a stagecoach and horses' manes rippling in the breeze while gulls circled above. There would be no sea wall, only dunes covered with rough grasses, and there would be no marks on the sand other than the imprint of horseshoes and thin ruts cut by coach wheels winding toward San Luis Pass. Years ago I might have been riding in that coach myself, riding somewhere further west to meet someone, some man who was expecting me. The wind blew my veil, my long skirt was tucked around my high-buttoned shoes, and my stays held me erect.

I left my romantic past, let it go curving on before me while slowing to look for a beer sign and red pennants. After passing two shacks, I saw the pennants and found Emmett slouched on some steps, his elbows planted on the porch, one boot heel resting in the sand, the other on the second step. They were his fancy boots, the ones with double row stitching outlining tan eagles on dark brown polished calfskin. His hair fell across his forehead. A little breeze pushed against his straw hat lying on the ground beside him. He didn't look unhappy, just lazy and drunk, completely drunk. He waved one arm in my direction as if to point me out to the tall man standing beside him.

I stopped at the steps. The man who had been waiting with him met me as I got out of the car.

"Hi. I'm Luis." He was the same height as Emmett, but his skin was darker, and he wore nothing but a swimming suit. Around his neck, on a thin gold chain, was a St. Christopher medal.

"Your friend—"

"He's not my friend." I waited twisting a sandal in the packed sand. Just seeing Emmett had made me angry. The hibiscus slipped lower over my ear. I pulled it free and let it fall.

Luis looked down at the crumpled red flower blowing away from us, then up at me.

"He's my cousin. Right now I don't much want to claim him."

He laughed. "Somebody needs to."

I climbed up the gritty steps, stooped down, and touched Emmett's shoulder.

"Celia, honey." He opened one eye. "You bring the beer?"

"You need some coffee. I can't take you home like this."

"Not going home." He wagged his head. "Going to Aunt Bertha's," he said with drunken exactitude, a strange reaction, but by insisting on certain details, he must have believed he remained in control when he was practically helpless. I'd seen other boys react the same way after drinking too much at fraternity parties.

"You know you can't go to Bertha's drunk."

"Who's drunk?" He peered down at his boots as if admiring them. "Feet sure are hot."

"Take your boots off."

He leaned over and began tugging at the heel of his left boot. "Let's go wading in that big old Gulf. Let's you and me go wading." He smiled at me as innocently as a spoiled child who'd decided he wanted to please himself in a particular way.

"Luis," he shouted, "come help me with these damned boots."

Luis didn't move. "I thought cowboys took off their own."

"Yeah." Emmett started laughing and pulling off the second boot. He threw them both toward the car where they landed in front of the fender, eagles nose down.

I got the thermos out of the front seat.

"Where's the beer?"

"I bet they already told you inside you had enough of that."

I looked up at Luis and he nodded.

"Come on Emmett. We're going wading." Luis, standing on the far side of him, put Emmett's arm around his neck.

I grabbed his other arm.

"Hey! I can do that." He lifted his arm slowly and let it fall around my neck.

Together Luis and I half carried, half dragged him to the sand's edge.

He was laughing to himself. "You know what, Luis? I like getting drunk just so I can hang around her neck."

"You're too heavy to hang on anybody." I kicked at him sideways to make him straighten up, but it was no use. He still lolled against me. We eased him down so the surf hit his feet.

"We should have put him the other way round. I 'd like to drown him." I looked down at Emmett. He seemed to have passed out. "Drunks are so boring."

"You have to do this a lot?"

"No . . . not really. He lives out in the country. His parents keep a pretty close watch on him except when he's off at school. I brought beer with me in case I had to lure him home. I wasn't sure how far gone he was." I looked back down at Emmett. He seemed content; his arms were outstretched where we'd let him fall.

"He needs to be out of the sun. I'll get an umbrella," Luis said. "There are some around here." He pointed toward a heap of poles and canvas stacked against the far wall of the bar, and before I could say don't bother, he'd walked away. I pried the thermos cap off, poured myself some coffee, took a few sips, and began trying to pour the rest of it in Emmett's open mouth.

He coughed and sputtered. "Goddamn! What are you trying to do, strangle me?"

I pushed the cup toward him.

"Hate coffee." He shoved it away with one hand.

"Emmett!" I was furious with him. He was absolutely too much trouble. I knelt beside him and grabbed both his shoulders.

With one arm he reached up and pulled me toward him.

"Leave me alone!" Panic overcame me. I hit his chest with both fists, but he held on.

"Never kissed you before. . . ."

"Let me go!"

"No."

He pulled me so close I could see darker flecks of color in his eyes.

The heavy yeasty smell of beer flowed all around us. I got an arm free and aimed at his face.

He caught my hand in mid-air. "Don't."

Raising my head, I saw Luis had walked up behind Emmett and was silently forcing the pole of the umbrella in the sand. Yellow shade flared above us. Emmett let go of me, reached for the thermos, heaved a great sigh, and poured himself some coffee.

I rolled away from him. I truly hated him at that moment, hated him so much I wanted to cry. At the same time I didn't want to cry, not in front of Emmett and Luis. I busied myself with my sandals, got them off and still holding onto their straps, ran west down the beach to the little rippling waves of the ocean that flowed everywhere and nowhere.

Chapter Three

I kept walking down the beach wishing for Tony Gregory even though it wouldn't have been any easier to deal with Emmett if he had been there. It would have been worse, lots worse. They would have despised each other on sight. Even so I tried to see him in front of me, blonde, fair as I was and blue-eyed too, we'd joked about kinship. His family was mostly Scandinavian while mine were, as far as anyone had traced them, French followed by generations of Scotch-Irish. When I wrote to him, I could visualize him better. Now, outside, he faded before I could get his face in mind. Why was he so hard to hold onto? I slowed to a walk swinging my sandals, one in each hand, watching the Gulf's trash wash up. There must have been a storm somewhere. Sargassum littered the shore in steaming rust-colored piles that straggled across the sand and filled the air with the medicinal smell of iodine reminiscent of falls, cuts on knees, and the stinging remedy used by adults all my childhood, of medicine cabinets, doctor's offices, of scabs and scratches, the unending novelty of one's own blood flowing and the need to staunch it immediately. Mercurochrome we sometimes called "monkey blood," but iodine remained iodine, the more painful sovereign remedy.

A sandpiper zigzagged in front of me scarring the sand as it ran. I hadn't told Emmett about Tony. Why should I have? He would never have understood me. I didn't understand my reactions myself. I guess I felt abandoned, loved and lost though not for any particular reason. I'd been the one who had to leave.

Away at summer school in Colorado for six weeks earlier that summer, I'd fallen in love with Tony Gregory, the guy with two first names, he called himself. My timing was terrible. I'd just finished my freshman year; he was in second year law school and unhappy. Family expectations pushed him. He thought he'd finish even if he hated law school. Just then it seemed that a number of the boys I knew went to school to please someone else. Maybe it was only the time. A lot of fathers came back from military service full of regret about time lost during the war and directed their sons to make something of themselves. Tony said his father was one of those.

The boys I studied journalism with had made their own choices. Many of them disparaged themselves. "Going to change the world, aren't we! Make it over. Tell the truth! Free the people!" They grinned mightily and falsely. Just beneath the self-mockery they carried on their crusades, stayed up all night chasing stories, meeting the campus paper's deadlines. Some worked part-time waiting tables in dorms or sorority houses or in small cafes around the campus, places already dependent on students' schedules. The *Daily Texan* was a scaled down version of a big city daily. We were in training.

"Trade school," was our name for the journalism program, and most everybody loved it. I wasn't altogether sold on the program. Sometimes news was immensely important; sometimes it was immensely trivial, and I couldn't decide if the two balanced. So much of the work was repetitious. How many days of the rest of my life did I want to spend reporting meetings, trying to find fresh angles about annual parades and rewriting other rewrites about the history of campus buildings? Maybe, I told myself, I found it hard to be enthusiastic because I was a novice who was only assigned the easy stuff. If I continued, I might get to do something worthwhile—and I liked the other journalism students. After the paper had been put to bed we sometimes met in a little dark bar near campus for a few beers. Nobody had the money for anything more or the time for a serious hangover.

Tony had both. He voted for Eisenhower and drank Scotch just as his father did. At the same time he vowed he really wanted to be a chef.

I couldn't understand why he didn't simply go ahead and go to a cooking school. If he couldn't find one in the U.S. he liked, wasn't there was one in France? It seemed to me that a twenty-three-year-old boy could choose to go almost any place to study anything. I'd had to persuade my father that, aside from my own lack of interest, girls didn't necessarily have to study home economics or elementary education, that I could be a reporter.

Tony only said, "They would never let me do it."

"Who has to let you?"

"My father. Always my father. And my brothers, but they're secondary. My mother doesn't give a damn as long as I do what my father wants— My family is a middle-class joke."

"My brother doesn't get along too well with my father either, but he doesn't want to be anything particular. He just despises school."

"Me too— Law school."

There was something more I knew. Law, to the Gregorys, was surely a cut above cooking no matter what fancy French schools might be available. To Tony's people in Omaha, a chef was the guy in the tallest white hat that forked the steaks.

For using his parents' money and hating their choice, Tony accused himself of indulging in the luxury of guilt, an odd idea to me. How could guilt be a luxury? It was always available. All I understood was he often drank too much. I began to drink more when I was with him.

Those six weeks in Colorado I studied history and philosophy; they made me sad because I was realizing once more there was no way I could help change the world entirely. Since the bombs had fallen on Hiroshima and Nagasaki, I lived under the same cloud of dubious hope as the rest of my friends. Born in peaceful times, we longed for them again, a paradox because none of us wanted to be stuck in the past.

Tony and I went to the opera in Silver City, to the dog races in Denver, rode the roller coaster that screamed out over a lake in an amusement park, went swimming in mountain lakes, tried the highs and lows of everything. Tony insisted, "Caviar and hot dogs!" It was frantic, exhilarating, and finally frustrating. I kept hoping to find a way to smooth over the edge of desire.

Tony reserved a motel room the last night I was in Boulder. We sat outside of it in his car and argued. Like most of the girls I knew, I feared pregnancy and had little faith in rubbers. I'd known girls at the university and in Leon High School who disappeared, didn't come back after Christmas vacation or left abruptly at mid-semester. We knew . . . all of us did, they were pregnant. In Leon when I was in high school, the school board had ruled against pregnant girls attending as if the mere sight of one might be contaminating.

Tony and I were as far apart as we could be on the front seat. My backbone rubbed the door handle on my side. He kept saying, "I don't see why not. We love each other. I want you."

"I want you too . . . but—"

"What?" He leaned toward me a little and I couldn't help meeting him in the middle. He'd already loosened my bra when I pulled away and began buttoning my dress. Tony had been initiated in a whorehouse somewhere. How expert he was I could only imagine, however he knew well how to slide zippers down, unbutton the smallest buttons, unhook the tightest hooks. Women's underclothes, though he liked to complain about various complications, were no mystery to him. He would even hook a bra up in the back if I asked. I didn't ask that night.

"I can't," I repeated.

"You want me, don't you?"

"Yes. I can't have you though."

Whirling around in my head was the memory of a girl I knew at school packing all her clothes in her parents' car that spring. She wasn't showing yet, but we knew she was in trouble. Her parents were in such a hurry to get her away, so frantic about her supposed disgrace, they hadn't waited long enough to let her slide her clothes on the metal rail hanging over the back seat. All of us who drove back and forth to school had one like it. Everything was slung in a heap under the railing, she got in between her father and mother in front, and they drove off. The white starched net of the petticoats we wore in layers beneath full skirts was so buoyant that hers rose and fell against the closed back windows like foamy waves imprisoned.

I still wanted Tony Gregory. I wrote him letters full of descriptions of my everyday life. I went here, did this, saw that and at the end of each one I said I missed him. My parents, I reminded him, had insisted I come to Galveston. They wouldn't send me back to Boulder anytime soon. His letters to me were brief: he was sometimes bitter about our need to live according to others' rules, and yes, he missed me too, but he had to go to school the rest of the summer. For once he was so sensible I wondered if I loved him more than he loved me?

I turned to look back at Emmett who was still lying on the beach, his legs straight out in front of him. Beside him Luis was digging in the sand with both hands.

A fat gray-haired woman holding her skirt up out of the water waded near me. A little boy clinging to her hem in back, began dipping it into the water behind her. She wheeled around.

"Let go, Jimmy. Here I try to keep dry and you're getting me all wet."

She grabbed up her skirt tighter in one hand and gave the boy the other.

By the time I'd walked back to Emmett, I saw he was asleep.

Luis looked up and said, "Don't worry. He'll be all right soon."

"Has he been drinking all afternoon?"

"Possibly. I stopped by around three. He was drinking then."

I knelt beside him and watched while he traced the outline of a figure in the sand. It was a face of some kind maybe. He'd added some small shells and sargassum all tangled like hair on top.

"What is this?"

"Nothing. If I had some plaster, I could make a casting."

"What would it look like?"

"Like it does here only reversed."

"A mask then?"

"Maybe."

Some quality in his voice made me study him. Until then I don't think I'd truly looked at him. He was just another guy Emmett had met in a bar, somebody helpful. Emmett seemed to have helpful friends around, other boys who would see he got home safely. Probably he attracted people who liked to look after others. Luis, when I saw him more clearly, was first of all, a beautiful color, a golden tan. His hair, short as everybody's, had been sun bleached, brown to almost blonde. He had a long face, a long nose, blue-green eyes. I thought him handsome, though a little odd and, in some undefined way, different. I kept looking at him while I told him we were in Galveston visiting an aunt and uncle. Once anyone began talking to Luis, I learned later, they began telling him things.

"Emmett's from Mullin, a little place near Leon where I live. I doubt you've ever heard of either of them. They're just Central Texas towns that exist for the people who live there, for them and their congressman, and...the newspapers if a tornado or a flood comes along."

"Oh?"

"Emmett goes to A&M. I'm at the university . . . in Austin."

He nodded. "I went to art school there."

"And now?"

He was staying with his father that summer. He'd been living in Mexico, in Guanajuato.

"I don't know it. I was in Cuernavaca once for a few weeks studying Spanish. It wasn't long enough to learn much. I'd like to go back."

Luis laughed. "At least you're trying. Most people here don't."

"I know. My father says we are provincial. He hates traveling himself, but he insists that I learn a foreign language."

"You like traveling more than he does then?"

"I don't know. Maybe."

At twenty I'd been moving most of my life. In forty-two we went with Mother to Florida to join our father. He lived on his post while we shifted from to rent house to rent house.

After my fourth school that year, they decided it was going to be a long war. Mother thought we'd be happier back in Nashville where my father had his last job, so we moved to an apartment near grandmother' house. When the war was over, my parents wanted a change. It was time to try Mother's state. We'd come to Texas to be the new kids in school again—this time in Leon. All the wandering seemed ordinary to me; staying put was strange. None of my new friends in Leon had ever moved except from one house to another in town and most of them had lived in the same houses all their lives. Still they had wanted to get away to college as much as I had.

Luis had drawn his knees up to his chin and was staring out toward the Gulf.

"We should go," I said.

"It's beautiful here in the mornings early. Why don't you come down?" Luis asked as if he were inviting me to his home.

I'd never been to the beach early in the morning. When we were living in Florida we were taken late in the afternoons, after two always.

"On weekdays," Luis insisted, "it's almost empty early. People come down from Houston and all the little towns around on weekends. Come Monday."

Emmett rolled and yawned. "God, I'm thirsty!"

I handed him the coffee.

He frowned at the thermos and put it beside him as if he meant to consider it later.

"How did you get so far down here?"

"Caught a ride."

"You hitch-hiked?"

"Naw. Fellows in the bar before brought me."

"And left?"

"I guess."

He handed the unopened thermos back to me.

"Come on, Celia. Don't be mad." He stood up, pressed bits of caked sand flaked off his jeans. "I'll even drive back." He winked at Luis. "Let's drink beer again sometime."

I collected Emmett's boots and carried them with me to the car knowing I'd better drive. He could do it; I wouldn't enjoy riding with him though.

Bertha was in the kitchen when I came in the side door. Emmett avoided her by going around the house to the front and running upstairs immediately. So I was left to explain to our aunt where I'd been in her car, not that she minded us using it. She'd told us to. But even if we were twenty and both in college, I knew she expected us to account for ourselves. Bertha was nosy but she also truly cared about whatever everyone under her roof was doing. Uncle Mowrey went through a debriefing in the afternoons when he came in. He didn't say much, silence being his habit, yet he generally had a little news for her, some comment on a person he'd seen or a call he'd received, and on hearing it, she would talk for five minutes or more reviewing first his whole day, then, at greater length, her own.

Delivering my account, I watched her face carefully. Except for the shape of it and the olive color, she hardly looked kin to the other Chandlers, to Estes, or Mother or Uncle Blanton. It was peculiar how brother and sisters could look so unalike. There was Kenyon, dark-haired like all the Chandlers, while I was decidedly kin to the Hendersons with my light hair and eyes the same blue as my grandmother's. Bertha's skin was badly wrinkled. Though smooth on her cheekbones, it fell in little lines under her eyes. Gray already, large bosomed, she was not pretty, nor according to earlier pictures, had she ever been. She was imposing, not dignified or stuffy but strong. With no children of her own, all the Chandlers, I supposed, were her children. The eldest certainly, Bertha remained the stoutest—she said so herself—and my father said, "the most decorated." She loved diamonds and wore them sprinkled about like raindrops in pins, a watch, earrings, rings.

They flashed on her fingers while she was busy picking out bits of shell from a bowl of fresh crabmeat.

"What was it this time, Celia?"

"The beach. I left you a note. I went down to get Emmett."

"No, that's not what I'm worried about. What is Emmett drunk on this time?"

I shifted from one foot to the other before sitting down in the chair across the kitchen table from her. "He's not terribly drunk. He drank some beer this afternoon." I dodged her question wondering at the same time why I bothered. Bertha could bear to hear the truth although she wouldn't like it.

"He's going to turn out just like Blanton if we don't watch him."

I'd seen Blanton once at his home in Laredo and three times at our house in Leon, all Thanksgiving visits. Though supposedly alcoholic, I'd never seen him drunk even if both Bertha and my mother vowed he was often. All the Chandler men drank. So did the women, though they drank a lot less. On holidays the men, my father joining them, settled in overstuffed chairs in my parents' big back bedroom to drink. They said they were staying out of the women's way in the kitchen. Actually Uncle Blanton and Uncle Estes hardly knew what to do with themselves inside. They talked about politics a little, commented on Southwest Conference football, spoke of livestock, of horses, weather—the long drought especially—the market for cows, calves, and sheep. I would overhear them when I was sent to call them to the table. Ice rattled in their bourbon, and their voices rumbled together slowly like bears' growling companionably in a nearby cave. Most of the time my father listened. He was an engineer and knew nothing about ranching. It took both uncles a long time to say anything much, yet he liked their talk. Nobody came to the table drunk.

"Aunt Bertha, do you really think Uncle Blanton drinks too much?"

"He always has. When he bought land down on the border, he stayed too much alone at first, trying to make a go of it, then he waited too long to marry. We used to hope he'd slack off, and he just grew into it. I see Emmett's inclined in the same direction."

"Maybe he's just trying it out, seeing what it does to him. Boys do that a lot at school."

"He'd be a little dumb not to know that by now." Bertha smiled and shoved her chair back. With one hand she reached for a spoon about to fall off the counter's edge behind her. Catching it just in time, she carried it with her over to the stove. She cooked in slapdash fashion, stirring pots just before they ran over or slightly after, pouring steaming food into bowls which barely held it. Jumbling spices on her shelves with sauce sticky fingers so the labels were barely legible, selecting each one with judicious pinches, moving lids, adjusting flames, she juggled her way to supper. Her meals were not timed since she seemed to rely on her nose to tell her when various dishes were done, yet food always seemed to be ready when everybody was hungry, and it was marvelous food.

"Celia, hand me those hot pads over there. Never can find them when I want them. And the salt. What did I do with the salt?"

Before I could point it out, her hand landed on the salt cellar.

I set the table and strayed into the living room to find Uncle Mowrey. He was sitting in his chair, his fat legs showing beneath *The Wall Street Journal*. Because he was an accountant and played the stock market with such success, the men in the family joked about picking up *The Journal* when Mowrey put it down just to see if he'd underlined anything. He didn't talk about his investments. In fact since he seldom spoke at all, his silences weren't threatening; they were puzzling. I'd asked my mother why he didn't talk, and she said he'd never had much conversation.

Bertha was teaching in Galveston when they met, and the first time he came to Mullin with her he was so quiet Uncle Estes thought maybe something was wrong with him. Around the Chandlers Aunt Bertha continued to do most of the talking.

Now, during my second visit, I wondered again at Mowrey's long silences. Was he half listening, half wandering in his own world as I'd done as a child? Was he resentful of everybody else's chatter? Slowly I began to understand that Mowrey depended on Bertha to do the talking in most social situations. She wanted to engage other people while he would only speak about what he knew. If a conversation moved to history, Mowrey might join it. Generally he talked to me about only one subject, Galveston, which he seemed to love more than any place in the world. Bertha once said he'd been planning to leave since he was nine years old but, of course, he never had.

I handed him a gin and tonic she had mixed. He accepted it with a noise made deep in his throat implying thanks, and looking up at me, he lowered his paper slightly.

"Uncle Mowrey, did Laffite really bury treasure here?"

"No one's sure. That's why everybody digs."

"But do you think he did?"

"I don't know. I think people want to believe it's there. Pirate treasure . . . something to hunt for. Kept Emmett busy all that visit." He smiled. "Laffite. . . . He's hard to pin down. Some of the old romancers saw him as a brave buccaneer taking Texas's side against the Spanish. Others remember Galveston began on uncertain ground…claimed by Mexico, by Spain, by the U.S. And islands were open to pirates. Laffite was the best known. He was a slave trader, something most people forget, and he traded whisky most probably. My guess is he was an opportunist, not particularly loyal to anyone. But people generally overlook that. Usually they remember he was a pirate who hated Spain and painted his house red. I guess we love rascals. They seem to get away with more."

Bertha called from the kitchen that supper was about ready and told me to holler at Emmett.

I did and when there was no answer, ran upstairs to find him asleep again. He slept on his back, one arm outflung, looking, even while sleeping, as if he could wake immediately like a wary animal on the edge of action.

I thought of my friend Claire who'd dated him. She'd told me, "Emmett's not for reforming. He kept me out till three drinking bourbon! I don't like bourbon! I don't even like to drink. I like drinking with Emmett. The trouble is I can't trust myself around him."

Claire wouldn't go out with him anymore. She was bright, practical, on her way somewhere, not to just anybody's bed, nor to Emmett's car's back seat. Well neither was I, yet I had to admit he was dangerous to me also. Even if I was sometimes furious at him, I was often attracted. And why this had to be, I couldn't begin to understand. All I knew was I had to avoid giving in. It looked like we'd have to go on living together while Aunt Bertha and I claimed kinship, and he ignored it.

I stood in the doorway and called his name. My fingers fell on the door's old heavily varnished oak frame, traced the small wooden grooves outlining it. The long twilight filtered through the shutters of the windows behind our two narrow beds divided by a strip of faded rag rug, washed over the white cotton spreads I'd pulled up to cover the pillows that morning. Emmett's boots stood toe to toe on the floor, his body sprawled aslant his bed, the ceiling fan whirred through the damp air. I saw it all so clearly, saw then that what seemed most forbidden could become what was most desired.

"Wake up, damn it!" I practically shouted at him, at myself.

Bertha seemed surprised when I said I would like to go to mass with her. "Are you sure? It's all in Latin. You won't understand a thing."

"I've been to Catholic churches before with friends. I don't mind not understanding. Look!" I showed her a little white straw pillbox. "I even brought something to put on my head just in case you asked me."

Face powder clouded around her shoulders as she brushed it off and settled her own red poppy covered hat on top of her frizzy curls. "At least in the Catholic Church, they appreciate hats." She checked to see if her earrings had been screwed on tight enough by shaking her head. "You're not to tell anybody in the family. They'll think I'm trying to convert you."

"I won't tell. Anyway . . . who would ask?"

"I don't know. Someone will. There's nothing bigger than family curiosity. I know. I've got it myself. Come on if you're determined to go. I never keep anybody away from church."

The Church of the Sacred Heart was a great blinding white building topped with a Moorish looking dome and two crenellated towers sprouting *fleur de lis* at regular intervals. Below a succession of arches outlined the entrance. Since it stood in the midst of tall palms, to me it looked more like a sultan's palace in a 1940's Hollywood spectacular than a church.

I was in a slippery state about religion, half scornful, half wondering, a fretful agnostic. Sitting quite still during the mass, I watched the priest and altar boys. Bertha, after handing me a printed translation of the service, had joined the ritual of adoration and supplication, kneeling and rising with the rest of the crowd. The church, white inside as well as out, its stained glass windows—pale blues, grays, greens and pinks—reflected the island's summer colors. "Harbor the Homeless. Ransom the Captives. Visit the Sick. Clothe the Naked. Instruct the Ignorant. Feed the Hungry. Give Drink to the Thirsty. Bury the Dead." The windows' black captions admonished us in clear English under pictures of small people dressed in what seemed to be medieval costumes following those instructions. I particularly liked, "Clothe the Naked." It seemed so immediate I imagined people carrying extra clothing whenever they went out just in case they found someone naked. Such straight forward, specific commands were strangely Puritan in a Catholic Church. There was not a single direction of the kind I was accustomed to such as, "Love thy neighbor." At the elevation of the host, I bowed my head yet refused to pray. To do so, I thought, would only be a temporary reaction to the waves of devotion I sensed moving around me. I would not be carried away, could not bend to the church's mysteries, or to my own needs; balkiness I recognized though I couldn't understand it.

Studying the backs of people's heads, I found I was searching for Luis and remembered his St. Christopher medal shining against his throat. How would he look from the back, especially if he had on a jacket? Still wishing vaguely that I might see him, I followed my aunt out of the cool church and waited for a moment with her under the arches before stepping into steamy sunshine. From the white oleanders, still wet with dew, emanated a smell I had previously associated with funeral flowers. The tall palms growing in front to the left and right of the main sidewalk, would have been a more suitable backdrop for a sheik, his robe flapping in the wind as he strode forward. New mass goers straggled indoors. Without turning I could hear the priest's voice droning, "*In nomine Patris. . . .*" Across the street Aunt Bertha pointed out a huge Victorian house, the Bishop's Palace.

Her head haloed by the stiff red poppies circling her hat, she took my arm as we strolled down the steps.

"Are you satisfied?" She asked.

"It's a satisfactory sort of church if you want ritual, I suppose. I don't know much about it."

"It pleases Mowrey. This morning when you were still asleep, he went to early mass. You're Methodist like your parents, aren't you?"

"I'm not sure now." I had never said that to anyone, but I kenw Bertha wasn't going to be shocked.

"Well, we all go though a doubtful time. When I was about your age—younger really—and living in Mullin I heard about hell every Sunday. I got tired of it. Every sermon started with a "Thou shalt not." Some of those 'shalt nots,' the little ones anyway, I was determined to try—to drink, dance, play cards. . . ." She laughed. "I didn't know why they have to make so much of little things. And there wasn't much choice in a tiny place like Mullin. Baptists . . . Methodists. . . . There wasn't a Catholic in town, not one in the area. Mowrey and I got married down here. Our priest has a drink with us when he comes over."

I wondered what Grandmother Chandler had to say about it, but Bertha only laughed and said she never talked to her about religion any more. "You can't drag everybody along with you when you go."

We walked on home to find Uncle Mowrey sitting on the back porch drinking coffee, the Sunday paper all around his ankles. Emmett was gone.

"Didn't say where he was going," Uncle Mowrey reported.

"To the beach, I guess," Bertha said. "There isn't much else open. Bars are closed on Sundays."

"Ah, Bertha—" He sighed and by that slight sound, I knew he sometimes disagreed with her. At the same time, it was plain he couldn't change her habits. It was one of those married people's sighs. I'd heard my parents make the same sound, half-yearning, half-acknowledging.

I was surprised then when Uncle Mowrey said, "How's the boy ever going to grow up if you and his mother know where he is all the time?"

Chapter Four

Luis was sitting at about the same place where I'd seen him before. I caught sight of him from a long way off and was glad to know the name of one person in the great blank space of the beach early in the morning. He seemed to be drawing something in a sketchbook; all his attention was bent toward an object I couldn't see. As I got closer I could watch his hand moving quickly, pausing, moving on.

When I stood beside him interrupting his gaze, he said, "Well, here you are," just as if he'd acknowledged Emmett or anyone else who came along. Putting his sketchbook aside, he looked up, "Come sit down."

"In a minute." I peered over his shoulder to see what he was drawing and found he'd been working on a picture of a water-soaked tennis shoe at the edge of the tide line. Everything seemed to wash up on Galveston's beaches. Sometimes there were clots of tar tangled in the seaweed, bits of net, cans and other debris.

"All this stuff. . . . Is it thrown overboard from ships or what?"

"Some of it floats up in the Gulf Stream all the way from Mexico. We get coconuts from beaches there or further south."

"From your part?"

"No. Guanajuato's in the mountains, near San Miguel, west a little. It's a colonial town. The Spanish mined silver there. It's built on the sides and in the valley of a deep canyon."

"It must be a lot cooler. Don't you hate to leave it in the summer?"

"It is beautiful. My father lives here though. I come up to see him."

"Where does he live?"

"In the Galvez."

"The hotel?"

"Yes."

I wanted to ask why, but something about the way he replied stopped me. He didn't want to talk about his father perhaps. "I think I'll get in," I said.

"Watch for jellyfish. They're out this morning." He got up. "I'll come with you."

I shuddered when the cool water lapped around my ankles but was determined to get wet all over at once so kept moving across the long shallow shelf out to the waves. Luis, much taller, stepped ahead of me. I couldn't catch up with him until we reached higher water. Even then he was a foot or so away. We rode the waves silently, purposefully, careful of the surf rising and falling, sometimes high, sometimes in quiet slow swells, varying without apparent pattern. It was easier to swim in the Gulf than in the Atlantic. Though cool in the morning when it hit the beach the water stayed fairly warm overnight, and the waves rocked gently.

"Look out!" Luis shouted.

Soft blobs of clear white bubbles drifted by my side. Luis caught me around my wrist with one hand and pulled me over next to him. He let go as the wave receded. Looking back I saw the white shiny mass lifted over a wave just behind us. Shaking a little, treading water, I wished I could be carried back to shore.

"I hate those things."

"Were you scared?"

"I can't stand to brush against jellyfish. I don't think I'd mind the sting as much as I'd mind the feel of them. Slimy!" The possibility of touching one made me shiver again. I started swimming in as fast as I could. Soon the long slopes of sand made it impossible to swim at all. Everyone save the smallest child had to walk a long way to get out of the Gulf.

Once back on the beach lying on a towel in the sun, conscious only of the warmth of the sun on my back and of Luis a few inches away, I forgot about the threat of jellyfish. Sitting up and pulling my feet under me, I looked over at him. His back was smooth and evenly tanned down to his waist; a pale line showed slightly where the elastic gave. Shifting my gaze to the water's edge, I watched a sandpiper tracking the ragged end of a wave, pecking now and then at pieces of seaweed. Further down the beach a woman began taking food out of a basket and piling waxed paper covered squares on an old army blanket. It was so early for lunch I wondered if she'd brought sandwiches for breakfast. I would like to know her, I thought. I would like to know anybody who preferred sandwiches to eggs and bacon.

Luis was so still he could have been asleep. I turned to him. "Don't you wish you could live on the beach with nothing but a pot to cook in and a spoon to stir with?"

"Two spoons," he said as he sat up and pulled the towel across his shoulders. "And an umbrella."

"You've got such a good tan I don't see why you have to worry about sunburn."

"It's inherited," he smiled slowly. "Partially."

"Well that's a help." I grinned at him and pulled my wildly clipped bangs down over my forehead. "I have to use my hair to keep the sun off, or I'll have terrible freckles."

"I'm half Mexican . . . on my father's side."

All I could think of was my father's reaction after we first met Uncle Blanton whose skin was even darker than Uncle Estes's or Mother's. I'd asked if he thought he looked Mexican, and my father had agreed he did. He'd warned me, however we'd better not mention it. Living mainly in Tennessee, I saw Mexicans only as people from Mexico, that exotic unknown country next to Texas. Prejudice against Negroes—I'd known since childhood—filled the air everyone breathed although some of that had worn away during the war. His service stripped my father of much of his. "We all have the same color of blood," was his final pronouncement on the subject, and I heard it young, years before I came to Texas. I knew he was right, but his view wasn't shared by all of the Chandlers or by many of the people we knew in Leon. Although there were few Negroes in

Colorado University's summer school, I'd worked with one who was reporter on the student newspaper and was relieved no one there mentioned his skin color.

Alone with Luis all I could say was, "You're lucky, you know. We have my father's side . . . back for generations, but I don't know much about my mother's family. Maybe somebody kept up with them, but nobody I know." I stopped myself, aware that I'd been chattering idiotically, filling in space in case I'd embarrassed him.

Luis looked at me in an amiable way as if he understood I was trying not to pry. "I don't mind being half Mexican. It gives me two countries."

"Don't you have to choose?"

"Citizenship? Yes. I chose the U.S. But I've still got two countries."

"Sometimes I think I do too. I was born in the South, and moved to the West. My parents decided it was time to try out Mother's state.

Luis laughed.

The West was still a foreign country, I felt, no matter how long I'd lived there . . . seven years, long enough for some people, maybe not long enough for me although I knew I felt at home in Galveston. It was a lot like the South because it was old and slightly worn. A lot had happened here; the houses themselves told you that.

For some reason, just as we'd discovered a small likeness I grew wary and wanted to get away. Until then Luis was only a boy, somewhat older than I, that Emmett had met on the beach, someone he'd stumbled across and introduced to me. The idea of simplicity was so seductive. My own life was a jumble, and here was Luis, the American-Mexican with a father he didn't seem to want to talk about and a mother too, no doubt, and his two countries. Everyone came with something, with strings, with ties. Tony carried all the Gregorys with him everywhere; I knew them in some ways better than they knew themselves though we'd never met. A girl friend gets all sorts of privileged information. Luis's, I sensed, would be even more complicated than Tony's. I could have excused myself. I could have left. But I didn't want to spend the rest of the day with Emmett, nor did I want to be completely alone. A part of me was already running through Bertha's and Mowrey's back gate, brushing past the white oleander bush, turning on the hose attached to the oak cistern, rinsing salt off with soft rain water. Then up the steps I would go and into the confusion of Bertha's kitchen. It would be hot; she'd probably already be cooking, getting something ready for supper ahead of time. I knew exactly what was waiting there. I chose Luis.

We spent the rest of the day together after taking Bertha's car back. He used the rainwater and shared the towel with me in what could have been one of those peculiarly public moments of intimacy. With Luis it was merely the usual necessity of getting rid of salt before going in. He picked up a neatly rolled bundle of clothes, and I pointed him toward the downstairs bath. Emmett, thank God, had gone out somewhere.

When I introduced Luis to Bertha she immediately said, "I know your father," she said. "Alberto . . . Alberto Platon. We see him out at the Balinese Room often."

"Yes. He likes going out there."

He said nothing more just then, but as I ran upstairs to change, I could hear their voices.

We ate lunch together at one of the piers near the shell shop. I looked for the Jamaican with his drum. He wasn't in sight. Where did he go when he wasn't on the seawall?

"He has a place," Luis said. "Three blocks or so back there's a house his relatives live in, I think."

"Is that a section for Negroes?"

"No, not in this older part of town. They're all scattered in with everybody."

I was so astonished I blurted, "That would never happen in the South."

"Really? It's been going on here a long time. Maybe because it's an island."

He folded himself back into his old MG. It was his mother's car she'd used only in town. She was dead, had been for three years. "Cancer," he said, just the one word, then added, "Of course she was too young. Anyone's too young to die of that."

'I'm sorry. It must have been . . . must be a terrible loss."

I wanted to comfort him and didn't know how. Why were there so few words to do this, especially when you haven't known the person who died and barely knew the person you were trying to sympathize with?

I brushed away the sweat running down the sides of my face. It was hot in the car on top of the seawall.

"I mean…you get over the worst but you do remember."

"Yes." He looked out toward the water glittering in the noon heat.

"It must be hard to be here, to be in Galveston without her."

He still wouldn't look at me.

"Sometimes it is." His voice was so low I could barely hear him.

He wiped sweat off his forehead with the back of his arm and began pulling out in the traffic along the seawall. Turning away from me, he scanned the street behind us.

Had I said too much? He'd trusted me enough to let me know about his mother. Could I know him better now?

He started driving toward the east end of the beach where we were going to catch the state ferry to Bolivar. We would ride over and back because, he insisted, we needed to get off the island for a while.

"Why? You leave Galveston, drive to Houston sometimes, don't you?"

"Sure. Over the causeway. I'd rather leave in a boat. What's the use of an island if you don't use the sea around it?"

Though I had crossed and re-crossed parts of the U.S., I'd never thought of an island that way. For me an island was a place removed, a place one could flee to, not a point of connection. I'd never been anywhere by sea. We climbed to the second level passenger deck above the cars. The ferry, an old one smelling of grease and gasoline fumes, rocked slowly across the bay accompanied by rattling ropes and metal pulls clanking against poles. Franklin gulls followed shrieking above us. They dipped to the water, skimmed the surface, then rose again filling the air with their greedy cries. Below the ferry's engine thumped like an overloaded old washing machine's. The water grew choppy, full of little upstart waves that made the ferry shudder as it moved in a long curving passage to the opposite shore.

Luis, in a soft white shirt and a pair of old jeans he'd pulled on at the house, leaned against the rail in front of me. The white shirt accentuated his darkness, his distance. At times anyone, even those who were close to me, seemed unknown. I'd caught Tony Gregory like that, looking away, cut off from everyone, a person totally apart, so separate he couldn't be reached. My father, Kenyon, Emmett, any man would, for minutes, become completely alone, completely themselves. So could any woman; men only seemed further away. Watching others, I would notice my own loneness. It came to me then that we all lived in small spaces, little territories which others occasionally crossed.

A sudden stiff wind puffed the back of Luis's shirt. He nodded toward a freighter weighted to the halfway mark on its waterline. From where we were, it was huge, its formidable black hull pointed to the open sea.

"They always look mysterious, don't they?" he said. "Probably carrying something like sulfur mined over in New Gulf. It's only going about the business of the world as usual."

The crossing from Galveston to an unknown coast made me long for a real ship, a real sea. These longings overtook me more and more lately. The most eventful trips I'd made had all been from one house to another, from one set of people to another set that had to be adjusted to. Even my trips to and from universities were necessary ones as were the family vacations I'd finally escaped and the obligatory trips back to Nashville. My mother and father returned infrequently now. Kenyon never wanted to go back, so I had been sent instead. Mother had traveled for pleasure, had taken off to unknown places, before the war. She and Aunt Bertha had been to Cuba and to England. My father poked around Europe for a year right after he finished college. Like them I wanted to know more of the world.

At the Bolivar landing we waited listening to motors turning over and watching cars plunging toward shore like awkward turtles. Children walked on a fragile looking pier near the landing, a dog lingered behind them to roll in the sand. At the end of the pier a group of men fished silently. One of them pushed his hat back on his head and studied us for a moment before turning his eyes back to his pole again. The rest, sitting two or three together, or standing almost motionless their heads bent toward the water or staring out to sea, made a jagged frieze against the sky.

After the last car was off and just before the others started on, there was a moment of calm broken only by gulls' screams and waves slapping. Bright sun fell on the gray beach, on the asphalt road leading past a grove of trees, the landing, the lighthouse at the other end of the bay. The two of us, dangling over the water, were suspended in light. I waited, happily dazed by heat and sun, content to be taken back to Galveston.

Emmett was away when I got home late that afternoon. Bertha didn't know where he'd gone. He'd borrowed her car and taken off.

"Maybe he went looking for you. He was upset about you being out with Luis. I wish youall would quit wandering off. I can't seem to catch the two of you together, and I want to introduce you to some young people."

"Why should Emmett care about me going out with Luis?" A little tired, wanting a shower and fresh clothes, I edged away from her toward the stairs.

"He said . . . He said he didn't like it because Luis is Mexican."

I turned to face her. "Half Mexican. What difference does it make anyway?"

"None," said Bertha. "That's what Mowrey tried to tell him. We've always had a duke's mixture here on the island . . . Jews, Mexicans, Irish, Scotch, Negroes, Italians, Germans."

I waited wondering how many other nationalities she'd name.

She was sitting at the kitchen table where she'd evidently just finished looking at part of the newspaper folded in her lap. Now she picked it up and began fanning herself.

"It doesn't matter to us, Celia, not to me, not to your Uncle Mowrey. But it does to Emmett."

"It's none of his business." I was so angry I could hardly speak. "What if I tried.... What if I told Emmett he shouldn't... he shouldn't date certain girls?"

Bertha's eyes widened. She slid her glasses over her nose and laid them carelessly, lens down, on the table.

"Earlene does that, doesn't she?" She smiled as if the fight between Emmett and his mother wasn't especially important. "I guess," she added, "he thinks he should look after you."

"Well he can think all he wants!" I turned my back on her knowing look. Lately I'd begun to notice there was, among the Chandler women, an unspoken custom; they told each other whatever their men thought, gave sharp attention to attitudes and ideas. And within the family, the men's opinions were important. Were they more important than the women's? I wasn't sure. Often everyone knew they were absolutely contrary. Aunt Earlene didn't care about horses—she'd seldom been on one—while Uncle Estes knew their bloodlines back some-times for three generations. Mowrey and Bertha, though both Catholic, went to different masses and regularly canceled each other's votes, or so Bertha said. There was no way of knowing about that. My father hunted and fished the year round while Mother, though she cooked whatever he shot or hooked, did not get near guns or tackle.

Leaving Bertha in the kitchen, I walked up the stairs slid-ing one hand along the banister's dark wood as I went. One day, if Bertha had her way, there would be no stairway. She and

Mowrey were getting too old to climb it, so the stairs would come down, and they would come down with them to live on the first floor after the guest bath had been remodeled and a shower added. The top floor would become an apartment with its own exterior entrance where renters would live or a visiting family might stay. The staircase that Mowrey's father had built, one put together with pegs, would go to Emmett for his own home—if he ever had one. Old people were always making plans like that. Grandmother Henderson wanted me have her silver goblets and her rings. A maiden aunt had already asked me if I'd take her bed. There was plenty of "This will be yours someday" kind of talk. It made me tired. I didn't want anything of anybody's no matter how badly they needed to leave their things to someone. I could just see myself sitting in my aunt's spool bed with a bunch of silver goblets in my lap and all of Grandmother Henderson's rings on my fingers. Why did one generation have to weigh the next one down so?

In the bedroom the ceiling fan was whining a lonesome song to itself. Shutters were still closed. The room was dark. One of Emmett's sheets trailed across the floor. I picked it up and began making his bed, as I usually did, not for him, I told myself, for Aunt Bertha who already had enough to do. When the sheet was securely tucked in, I threw the shutters open. All up and down the street I could glimpse people sitting on front porches waiting for dusk and supper. I sat down on the side of my bed and began unbuttoning my shirt wondering why I'd come to Galveston. Bertha had accused me—without saying so exactly—of ignoring Emmett. And she was right. We were still kin, of course. Ever since we moved to Texas the Chandlers had claimed us. We went to see each other, spent holidays together, called each other "Cousin," "Aunt," "Uncle," "Grandmother." And here was Emmett who refused to act kin to me while to Bertha he was only acting like a protective cousin. No shame was involved as far as he thought about his reactions, which wasn't far. And here I was within reaching distance every night, refusing to have anything to do with him even in the daytime.

I didn't want Emmett. Nothing but shame was involved for me.

Supposedly I was protected by those open doors, by Aunt Bertha and Uncle Mowrey sleeping ten or twelve feet away. I didn't feel protected. Now Bertha, in her strange innocence, had let me know Emmett was jealous of Luis. What a hopeless muddle! If I told her Emmett tried to kiss me when he was drunk, I'd probably be blamed for attracting him.

Late that night the screech of tires against the front curb woke me. Emmett was trying to park Bertha's big Chrysler in front of the corner streetlight where no one was supposed to park. Kneeling at the window at the head of the bed, I tried to see him. He must have taken a long slide across the front seat to open the door. I watched him fall with one hand out-stretched to the sidewalk. Behind him the door swayed open leaving the inside light glowing. The back of his shirt was split. He looked like he'd been rolling in dirt. Holding onto the slender limb of the nearest oleander, he struggled to a sitting position. I waited expecting to hear him slam the door. He was within easy reach of it, but the door no longer existed for Emmett. His head fell forward on one arm.

I got out of bed, and without stopping to put on a robe, ran downstairs. Better to leave the porch light off, I thought, and kept going down the porch steps. Bits of oyster shell on the sidewalk scratched my feet. Afraid we'd be seen, I pushed the car door too, then gave it a final quiet shove. Bending down to Emmett, I smelled horses, whisky, and dust.

"Come inside."

"Can't."

"You got this far. Come on."

He lifted his face and I caught sight of a scratch on his cheek.

"You hurt?"

"No. . . . Yes." He touched his cheek with one dirty finger as if he was making sure the scratch was still there.

"Where else?"

"All over."

I knelt beside him. "Emmett, where have you been?"

"Riding the bucking broncos." He tried to grin and touched his cheek again.

"Rodeoing?"

"Yeah. I got thrown."

"Where was the rodeo?"

"Texas City ... somewhere outside Texas City."

"What are you going to do next?"

He raised his hand again as if to touch his cheek. Instead he traced the curve of my chin with the tips of his fingers. "I don't know for sure."

"Well, come on. We've got to get you in. I'll help. Come on now before you wake up everybody."

He seemed more tired than drunk, but I couldn't be sure. I put one of his arms around my shoulders, slowly got him to his feet, and began directing him carefully toward the front walk. Before I could lead him there, he veered away to the little three-foot high front fence and tried to climb over it. His boot caught on the pointed arrow top of the iron railing leaving him wavering on one foot. I bet it wasn't the first time somebody had tried to step over that little fence.

With some effort I managed to pull him loose. "Where are you going? Are you crazy? Come on, Emmett, this way." I tugged at him, but he was too heavy.

His boot heels ground in the crushed shell as he pivoted around and stood in front of me. "Caught you."

"No!"

He held me against him with both arms. His belt buckle scraped against my stomach. Laughing, he bent his head down.

"No!" I kicked his legs and was amazed at his sudden strength. "Let go of me. I don't want you. I don't want anything to do with you. You tear up everything you put your hands on, even yourself." The crushed shell was cold and prickly underfoot, and I began to feel cold even while Emmett held onto me. He seemed to be studying me while trying to understand but at the same time was unwilling to believe what I'd told him.

"Listen," I tried again. "I don't belong to you, and I don't want to belong to you."

He let go of me but kept one hand on my shoulder. "You don't know what you want, Celia." His mood shifted to drunken seriousness.

"Well who does? Leave me alone now."

"All right." He sat down on the porch steps.

I got inside, clicked the porch light on, then started upstairs so fast I almost collided with Aunt Bertha waddling quietly down.

"What is it this time?" She asked slowly as if she were talking in her sleep.

"Whisky . . . rodeos and whisky. Saddle broncs," I added, determined to tell her everything this time. I paused for breath.

"My Lord!' Aunt Bertha started to cross herself, dropped her hand, and settled in a heap three steps from the bottom directly behind Emmett on the porch steps outside. I climbed the stairs past her and glanced back at both of them sitting, Bertha in a faded blue cotton robe staring down at Emmett's torn shirt and his head outlined by the bright yellow porch light where the moths had already begun flying in their futile circles.

The next morning the house was extra quiet. I didn't know how Emmett got upstairs. Maybe Bertha helped him. More than likely he wasn't really as helpless as he'd acted. When I went down for breakfast, he was apparently still in a sodden sleep, a pillow pulled over his head which he'd turned to the opposite wall.

Bertha made no comment about the night. Uncle Mowrey winked at me as if to say he knew something was going on and we should both keep quiet. I took the back section of the paper to read. When the mail came, there were two letters for me from Colorado. I opened Tony's first. He spent most of a page complaining about a course, one called Civil Procedure, which he'd decided to take during the summer session since this would bore him only six weeks rather than thirteen.

"It's worse than trusts, which was made up of dusty volumes and ancient rules. Procedure is just more rules and how and when you do everything. It's nothing but a set of obstacles. Right now we're studying discovery—interrogations, depositions, stipulations, requests for admission. Sounds like a long, stupid curse, doesn't it? For every rule there's an exception, so all this time you're locked in a maze with this guy droning on and wiping his glasses with his handkerchief all the time. You get so sleepy you wish he'd drop his glasses."

Despite this I knew he'd make a good grade. Tony enjoyed griping. At the same time he knew he was competing with every other law student in his class. No matter how much he told me he hated law school he would still come out on top if he possibly could. Competition was what interested him. He didn't say he was lonely. He barely mentioned missing me. The letter was signed "Love." I doubted he meant it. I didn't know why I thought so. It was only an intuition. Tony didn't spend much time in any letter telling me how he felt about us. Maybe he didn't know how.

The next letter from Alicia Dorman, my friend from Dallas who had stayed in Boulder for the second six weeks of summer school, was far more revealing. "Tony," she wrote, "is seeing a lot of Judy again evidently. I've run into them at Tulagi's and on campus." Judy Wapping was an old girlfriend of Tony's. I'd guessed that might happen. Why did my worst premonitions have to come true? I tore her letter in small pieces and put it in the garbage can behind the house, no way to treat a letter from a friend, but I couldn't take a chance on anyone else finding out. Tony's letter I folded and stuck in the pocket of my shorts to hide in my suitcase later. I'd write Alicia first and thank her for news I detested getting. No, I'd write Tony first, let him know I knew he and Judy. . . . I wrote Tony and tore up the letter. What if I didn't like him seeing Judy! I wasn't there.

What right had I to make such demands? None, of course.

I wrote Alicia a sensible note about the silliness of being jealous, put it in the mailbox two corners away, and turned back toward the house feeling reasonable until the image of Tony and Judy walking hand in hand across the Colorado campus outraged me again. That was all I allowed myself to imagine, and still I was so miserable and so angry I walked right past Aunt Bertha's and Uncle Mowrey's house dreaming of flights to Boulder.

That afternoon Aunt Bertha, who still had said nothing about Emmett's behavior, invited Roby Chilvers over. He arrived with two girls, Jane and Leslie, and another boy, Marion.

"They all go to UT, Emmett. I'm sorry. I don't know anyone with children at A&M."

"That's all right," he said. "You might of waited a day or two though." Bruises were showing on his face, and he was moving slowly.

I didn't understand why he had to keep on fighting, throwing himself up against walls of every kind as if he were still about fifteen. What would I have done if I'd been Emment? I couldn't imagine having Aunt Earlene for a mother or Uncle Estes for a father, pleasant as he was, nor did I believe Emmett's problems were all their fault.

"I couldn't know you'd go off and half kill yourself at the time I was arranging this for you. I guess you'll just have to manage." Aunt Bertha smiled at him.

He smiled back at her carefully; obviously he was trying not to move his swollen cheek.

I knew some sort of agreement had been reached. Probably Aunt Bertha wouldn't talk to Uncle Estes and Aunt Earlene if Emmett did as she asked. He needed distraction; she'd provide it. For her silence, he would play at being agreeable.

That afternoon we went swimming with Bertha's group. She'd wanted to send us to the country club. Roby talked her out of it. He had the amusing, easy manner of someone used to getting his way. "We can't have you sending the whole pack of us out there. What sort of hospitality is that! We ought to take Celia and Emmett to the old Galvez. They have a good pool."

"And a good bar," Jane added.

Slow talking, smiling, she seemed as easy going as Roby. Both of them had dark honey-colored blonde hair and were about the same height. They made a pair.

Bertha didn't object much. Marion's father, I later learned, was one of the owners of the hotel. He owned a great deal of Galveston real estate, though no one mentioned it. Marion was dark-eyed and pudgy, the reverse of Leslie who was slim and laughed a lot. They weren't a pair in any way.

Emmett said he didn't care where we went as long as we stayed away from saltwater. It was one of the few remarks he made that afternoon. He meant for us to believe he didn't want salt on his cuts, but I began to wonder if he didn't know how to swim and was embarrassed about it. Mullin was large enough to have a high school but too small to have a swimming pool. He hadn't been to any of the summer boys' camps on the Guadalupe though he might have at least learned to dog paddle in one of the ranch's tanks. They were all dry now. Even during ordinary weather they dried way down, were apt to be infested with water moccasins, and rimmed with cow plops. The only other large wet places were windmill water storage tanks, too small to do anything except float. If Emmett couldn't swim, I doubted he could float and if he couldn't do something, I was beginning to learn, he usually scorned it. That afternoon, without saying much, he established himself in a deck chair with a drink then fell asleep under a wide awning near the pool. He looked out of place there with his hat half over his face, his legs stretched out in jeans when the rest of us had on bathing suits.

"Hard night?" Roby nodded toward him.

"I guess so. He got involved in a rodeo somewhere outside Texas City."

"I've never been to one." He looked as if I'd just given him a gift he couldn't wait to open.

"I haven't been to one either," Jane said.

"Let's go!" Roby's voice rose.

Marion agreed immediately.

It was such a dumb idea I stared at the three of them, got up, and jumped into the pool.

Leslie was already in. "What was Roby saying?'

"He wants to go to a rodeo. I don't know why. Once you've seen one, you've seen them all."

"I've never seen one," said Leslie.

"Oh God!" I did a surface dive. The water was almost as warm as the Gulf's. The hotel, covered with pale orange stucco and a darker orange tile roof, faced the seawall. It had an air of twenties opulence. Waiters in white jackets carrying trays with elaborate care brought drinks. Though he was obviously the youngest one there, Marion signed for everything. No one else came to the pool. It was like being at a country club only less crowded.

I wondered at this and asked Leslie if everyone staying at the hotel had gone to the Gulf to swim.

"I don't know. I guess so. Or maybe Marion had them put up the sign saying *CLOSED*. He usually does when he's here." She laughed and swam across the pool.

What did the people who'd paid to stay there do? They were strangers, tourists on vacations, unaware that an owner's sons took special privileges. Wouldn't the manager, when somebody else wanted to swim, move the sign finally? Or was the hotel's staff accustomed to Marion's pushy habits? Maybe he, like Emmett, was trying to cover up a weakness. Emmett didn't want anybody to laugh at him. I flipped over on my back to gaze at the blank blue sky. I liked that pool, liked its quiet emptiness, the breeze blowing in from the ocean just across the street. There weren't many cars on the boulevard that day, so there was little traffic noise. Drifting aimlessly I raised my head now and then to hear gulls' cries, wind-rattling palm leaves, clinks of glasses on heavy glass-topped tables. Many of the hotel's windows overlooked the pool, yet they were set back so far there was no feeling of intrusion. Slowly I began to hear the murmur of surrounding voices and began swimming again. When I reached the side of the pool near him I heard Roby chanting, "Let us arise and go now!"

Jane sat on the edge nearby, her legs in the water, a Tom Collins in hand. "Roby," she said in a lazy drawl, "you are too much! We just got here."

I pulled myself up out of the water and sat down beside her. "He's ready to go?"

"Roby likes to do things, likes for us all to do things." She raised her eyebrows and drank.

Marion, standing directly behind us, pushed me into the pool. I wondered why he'd bothered and decided he must be bored. Swimming to the opposite side, I climbed out, walked over, and sat down by Roby to tell him there was no use carrying on about the rodeo. We couldn't arise and go to one since they were held generally at night in the summer and usually on weekends.

We went to the rodeo the next Saturday—all of us together—because Roby wanted go. No one but Emmett wore boots. None of them owned a pair, and I'd left mine in Leon. Everybody had on blue jeans and loafers except Marion who'd stuffed himself into a pair of white cotton trousers.

"He never knows what to wear," Leslie said. "Most of the time Roby has to tell him. Otherwise he'd wear a derby hat and a bathing suit to a football game. Wouldn't you, Marion?"

Everyone laughed, even Marion who evidently didn't like it but was used to being teased.

We drove across the causeway to a dusty little arena outside Texas City, arrived between events, and found a small crowd scattered over sagging gray bleachers. The Galveston group laughed at the sight of these people gazing so intently toward the empty space in front of them. They laughed at everything. We climbed on the bleachers and found seats. Emmett sat apart again, his elbows on his knees, his hat on his head. We were all steadily drinking beer from big paper cups.

"Oh, my God!" Roby exclaimed when the barrel races began. "What are they going to do now?"

"They ride around the barrels in figure eights. Girls do it. They ride for time."

"Have you ever—?" Roby asked.

I looked over at Emmett wondering if he was thinking of Doris Lacey. He was staring blankly toward the arena. He wasn't missing anybody.

I shook my head in answer to Roby. "Emmett's the one that rides, remember?"

"Yeah. What does he ride?"

"Saddle broncs."

"And falls off."

"Sometimes." I almost felt sorry for Emmett although he wasn't really paying attention to any of them. Every once in a while Jane would take his cup and refill it with beer when she was refilling hers. Roby had stowed a cooler full of cans in his car's trunk.

"What a lot of dust!" Marion, sitting by Roby's far side, coughed.

It was a scruffy little rodeo. There was no band, no real announcer, just a man with a mike, and not many people watching. The bleachers were so full of splinters they must have been sitting out in the rain for years. Where did they get the stock? I turned to ask Emmett. Where had he gone? He'd promised me he wouldn't ride, had complained he was still too sore.

I stood up and stared toward the pens where the horses and bulls were kept. Yes. There was Emmett in his green plaid shirt, his straw hat which, like his winter Stetson, had been steamed and shaped according to his instructions. Shaping a hat was a ritual performed in the store every time he bought a new one. He took better care of his hats than he did of himself.

Jane eased over next to me. "He's going to ride, isn't he?"

"I don't know. Maybe he's just looking at the stock. He's still pretty sore from riding last weekend." I sat back down. It looked as if he was going to ride after all, and if he'd decided to, there was no way I could stop him.

He was the third one out of the gate.

"My God, what is he doing to the horse?" Roby asked.

"Spurring him. It's part of it. They have to rowel the horses to make them buck."

He clung to a small dun-colored quarter horse that was doubled up under him. The number 251 showed black against a square of white on back of his shirt. The dun jolted up, then down, and up again. Emmett lasted one minute, forty seconds according to the man with the mike. "Too bad, Buddy," he added in the off-hand way rodeo announcers generally did.

Emmett lay sprawled in the dirt. I hoped he was conscious. Marion said, "Is he going to get up?"

Roby looked at him with his mouth open mocking him. "Of course, he is! For God's sake, Marion!"

Leslie handed me another cup of beer. "You want to save this for Emmett? I bet he's really going to be sore now."

I was furious at him for hurting himself again, for being such a willing fool.

"No," I said, "I don't want to reward him."

"Here," said Jane in her lazy voice, "give it to me. I'll save it for the boy."

The two of them spent the rest of the night getting drunk together, first hilariously—Jane wore Emmett's hat at this stage—then sadly. She sat in the back seat on Emmett's lap and cried while Roby drove us all back to Galveston.

He seemed to be sober when we all knew he wasn't. He drove almost normally, a little too carefully, the way old men drive—sitting up straight, shoulders slightly hunched—staying well on his side of the road. Sitting beside him, I could see how far away he was from the dividing line. Occasionally, when he wobbled toward it, I poked him gently with my elbow as Leslie had told me to.

"You'll have to do it, Celia. Whoever sits next to him has to. It's the only way we ever get home alive."

Marion, only a little tight, was on my other side looking out the window most of the time. At least Emmett hadn't insisted on driving.

I could hear him patting Jane's back and murmuring, "S's all right."

"No," she sobbed, "It's never going to be all right!" and cried some more.

"Why is she crying?" I craned my neck to ask Leslie in the back seat beside Jane and Emmett.

"I don't know. I never know." For once Leslie wasn't laughing.

"She's just a crying drunk," Marion said, as if repeating a judgment he'd heard before.

By the time Roby stopped at Jane's house, Emmett had grown morose, and she was trying to comfort him. We left them sitting on the curb together.

"It's where she generally wants to be left." Roby said.

"Outside?" I asked

"Her parents drink an awful lot. They don't think she should." Leslie answered.

"You mean they drink all the time?"

"Weekends mainly. They're weekend drunks. How will Emmett get home?"

"Somehow," I said. "He always gets back somehow." I was only pretending to be blasé. I wondered how he'd get home too.

On the way to Aunt Bertha and Uncle Mowrey's Roby drove by the seawall. When we passed the shell shop, the Jamaican was out front playing his tall steel drum. The zigzags he'd painted round it showed in the dim light.

"Do you know him?" I asked.

"Tom-Tom? He's been here every summer the past few years," Roby said. "He comes and plays. People give him money. He's just one of the people who float up now and then. We get lots of floaters."

A fast beat rose and faded as we went by. No one was standing around him. He seemed completely absorbed in the rhythm. Behind him a quarter moon sailed the horizon above the sea.

Chapter Five

Aunt Bertha, watchful at first, hadn't even wakened when I came in that night late from the rodeo, nor did she seem to notice that Emmett didn't get home until just before sunrise. She merely nodded and asked no questions when I left to meet Luis. Often he came by for me and delayed leaving to sit in the kitchen, drink coffee, and tell us both about Mexico, or to talk to Aunt Bertha about food. There were so many different kinds of peppers, he said. His mother had used some, jalapenos and serranos mainly, but he'd had to learn how to cook others after seeing them in the market. Food in the interior was nothing like Tex-Mex. Aunt Bertha got so interested I thought she would make him recite recipes before we could go. Around most people, but particularly with the older ones, Luis listened intently as if he really wanted to learn anything they might tell him. And it seemed to make no difference if they were old fishermen or my family. Watching him with Aunt Bertha, I felt my own impatience fade a little.

This time I decided I'd walk to meet him. The seawall was only five blocks away, so I went past all the little raised cottages standing on tall beams, hopefully above water level during storms. Their porches, empty in the mornings, would be filled after five—with men mainly since the women would be inside cooking supper. When Uncle Mowrey and I passed by, he'd nod and the men, sometimes holding children in their laps while talking across their porches to other men would say, "Evening," and nod back. Framed by curling gingerbread trim or plain white square posts, they were snapshots of other lives.

Their wives worked in smaller hotter kitchens than Aunt Bertha's. They had no time for strolls to the beach, nor, except for weekends, would they be sitting on their porches when we came by. Were they at home all day, or did they work somewhere else—in other people's houses, in stores downtown? Mother stayed at home and liked it. But she was in her fifties and had moved so often, she was happy to be in her own house. I meant to have a career even though I didn't quite know how. I'd just begun working on the *Daily Texan*. Someday, if I stayed with it, I might be a full-time reporter on a big city daily.

Walking along I stopped now and then to slide bits of oyster shell out of my sandals. I'd gotten used to meeting Luis at his favorite points on the beach. Aunt Bertha would have loaned me her car, I knew. I wanted to walk, to know the place better, I'd told her. What I didn't tell her was I wanted to keep Emmett away from a chance meeting with Luis. He wouldn't walk anywhere. If I borrowed the car, he might say he needed a ride some place and insist on going with me. Depending on his humor, Emmett acted some days as if he'd decided he needed to follow me everywhere.

Once when I was leaving to walk to the library, he insisted on driving me and waiting outside in the car while I went in.

"You could come too," I offered.

"What for?" He stayed in the car and complained when I returned, "Why do you have to read so much?"

"Why do you have to read so little?"

He shrugged. Silently staring forward, he drove me back to the house. I gave up trying to get him to say a word the rest of the afternoon.

Luis was never sullen, seldom irritable. As I approached the jetty near the east end of the island, I picked him out, sitting slightly back from the rows of men and women fishing off either side. As usual he was a part of a scene yet isolated within it while sketching some seemingly insignificant element. I found he would draw anything—shadows, two upturned cockle shells full of sea water, a pile of trash washed ashore, bones, people's backs, hands, buildings under construction or being demolished. He seldom drew faces, not because they didn't interest him, but because he didn't like to stare at people he didn't know. He would draw figures from a distance and he'd used models, as every student had, in art school.

He looked up, waved, and in a moment I joined him. Picking our way carefully, we stepped around a confusion of buckets, lines, bait, and people; whether sitting or standing they leaned out following the angles of their poles. I stopped to stare out past them to the open sea, so green and rough in the distance. When I turned back to look toward the beach, I saw two boys around seven or eight playing with two club-shaped gray fish, flipping them over by their tails in the sand, letting them struggle toward the water and pulling them back again just as they reached it. Tiring of this, they jerked the fish up and swung them heads down in the air watching them writhe. When they hung still, the boys slapped their bodies together until they wriggled once more.

I watched amazed at the toughness of the fish and wanting to yell at the boys to stop torturing them.

Luis hadn't noticed, so I asked, "What kind of fish are they killing?"

He looked toward the boys. "Horrid, aren't they. Those are small sharks. Someone up here probably caught them. Everything's hauled up on a jetty—sheepshead, smelt, sharks like those kids are beating up, crabs, sting rays. People here call the rays devil fish." He made a wide diamond shape using both his thumbs and forefingers. "This is what they look like, and they have a long whiplike tail with a barb in it. Most of them are poisonous. Hurts if you get stung. On the Mexican coast they're called mantas, I guess because they can get as big as blankets. I've seen old pictures of huge rays like that caught in Galveston, some of them bigger than the men who caught them."

I thought I'd never want to swim in the Gulf again and said so.

"Don't worry. They post warnings when schools are sighted."

"What about the ones nobody sees?"

"You don't see all the cars when you cross a street sometimes."

In front of me a man pulled what looked like a catfish off his hook by gingerly placing his finger around the fins on the side and back. "You got to watch how you do this," he said while looking up at me from under the bill of his cap. His teeth were brown with tobacco stains. "My wife stepped on one yesterday, and it sliced her instep. She's sick all over today. Poisons the whole system." He pulled up a stringer full of fish and laid his catch on the black asphalt-covered walkway. They stayed still while the catfish was attached. Lowered to a bucket in the water, the whole silvery bunch wriggled and pulled against the hooks.

My father hunted and fished. So did Kenyon. I couldn't say why I cared about the boys on the beach and their mindless cruelty or the fisherman brutally saving his catch. It was a puzzle to me, for nature alone could be just as aimless, just as cruel. Luis agreed although he didn't seem to mind the doubleness of things the way I did.

We walked on toward the open sea side by side. He seldom touched me, nor did he look for excuses to hold onto me either, a relief since Emmett was such a grabber. Had someone hurt him terribly, or was he a person who simply didn't need to touch others often? Tony . . . with Tony it had seemed natural to hold hands and just as natural for him to put his arm around my shoulders. Looking down I saw the tar had been worn away toward the lower end of the jetty. The concrete we were walking on was partially covered with patches of slippery green moss. My sandals were already wet. Automatically I reached for Luis's hand. Water dashed up against the walkway, and quickly oozed out again. A misstep could send us sliding down to enormous black-speckled pink rocks haphazardly piled on both sides. They didn't look like any other rocks I'd seen in Galveston.

"Where did they get all these?"

"The granite? Those are ten-ton blocks of it. They were dumped here before the seawall was built. I've forgotten where it's from." Luis shouted above the crash of the waves.

By now wet almost to my waist, I was hypnotized by the dizzying, curling waves smashing against the rocks. Every step we took, even the most tentative one, seemed to me to be in opposition to their tremendous force.

I looked over at Luis who was ignoring the spray. Of course he was taller.

"The water—" I shouted and gestured toward the spray with my free hand.

"Look up. Keep your eyes on the signal light out there." He pointed to a stubby piece of dark metal poking up at the end.

"We aren't going to walk out all the way, are we?" I wanted to turn and run to shore, but warned myself not to. Slipping on the oozing moss would be so easy. I grasped his hand harder.

"Afraid?"

"Yes," I didn't mind admitting. "Have you walked out there?"

He nodded. "I like to go to the end. The surf's too high today though."

I turned back gladly and let go of his hand as soon as we reached the dry section of the jetty.

The car's black leather seats looked so hot I half wondered if steam would rise when I sat down. Luis slid under the wheel without comment. The old black MG with its storage box on back collected sun and held it even though the top was always down. Heat didn't bother him. Cold did. It was cold in the mountains in Mexico in the winters, he'd said. We drove away from the jetty past the ferry landing where a single black and yellow striped wooden bar marked the abrupt end of land. One ferry was being loaded. The other would be coming from the opposite shore. Shifting gears down, Luis made the MG climb the slanting seawall. Behind it there was a bit of lowland where remains of World War II gun emplacements were standing on high ground. Uncle Mowrey told me they were built to guard the sea approach to Galveston Bay. Their jutting gray cement shafts and empty rectangles of long gone doors were slowly being camouflaged by grass. Luis stopped without explanation, as he often did, and we pushed ourselves up to sit on the backs of the seats.

Past the fortifications the bay circled around the island. Where I could no longer see water, a few tall masts and smoke-stacks indicated wharves. Straight ahead rose the white dome of the Church of the Sacred Heart. "Harbor the Homeless," I thought. "Instruct the Ignorant." What I needed was instruc-tion on breaking silent barriers between people and I could find none. I had to feel my way with Luis, to trust intuition. By my side was the beach sweeping back in a curve waiting to meet the sea. I looked once more at the mass of concrete with its grassy green cover.

"Do you suppose they're like that all over the world . . . wherever there's a beach?" I asked.

"Something like that. The D-Day beaches must be full of old wrecked bunkers and barbed wire rusting."

I tried to imagine soldiers in other beach outposts waiting to meet invaders, the menace of quiet while men crouched in the earth, their eyes straining toward sky and sea. "Did you know anybody in the war?"

"My brother. He was killed on Guam." He looked down at his hands lightly folded in his lap.

"I'm sorry."

"He was a lot older, and I didn't know him well except he . . . he was a kind of hero. I wanted to be like him when I grew up. He loved this." He leaned his head toward the beach. "Sometimes I think of him out in the Pacific . . . on that other beach. He was buried there. My mother couldn't stand it. She wanted him brought back home. For a long time she wouldn't believe he was dead, even after the official notice came, she wouldn't believe it. When she started believing— She had cancer when she started believing." He stared straight ahead over the small windshield. "And I didn't grow up to be like him in the least."

I was reminded of a small boy on-stage reciting something he'd learned by heart, fearful of stopping for a second, fearful if he did, the next line would be forever lost. At the same time I felt the next line was well learned, and he would know it all of his life. The way his voice fell told me he wasn't simply mourning the loss of his brother and his mother. He was trying, in an oblique way, to tell me about himself . . . that he wasn't in the least like his brother. . . . Why did he think he should be?

I started to say something about Korea, that everybody knew it wasn't at all like World War II, that he hadn't missed an opportunity to prove himself there, then said nothing. What did I really know about him and his missed opportunities? He wasn't talking about not being a soldier. There was something else, but I couldn't ask, couldn't say "What is it, Luis? What is wrong?" He didn't want me to. I was certain of that.

"What about you?" He asked shaking his head a little as if beckoning another child to come out of the wings and take his place.

"There was my father, but he didn't go overseas. They kept him in the U.S. to train troops. One aunt had a husband stationed in India with the Air Corps. He caught lots of strange fevers but he came home. None of my Texas uncles served. Too young, too old, or busy raising cattle. My family's totally divided, half in Tennessee, half in Texas."

"Mine is simple here . . . just me and my father. There's all my mother's side. They live in Houston. In Mexico all my father's family is scattered around."

"Near Guanajuato?"

"No . . . over closer to Guadalajara most of them. I see them on holidays mostly. Mexicans are like southerners a little . . . all those connections. They keep up with each other. I have more cousins than I can count."

"Well, at least you don't have an Emmett."

"Maybe I wouldn't mind somebody looking after me." He smiled.

"Oh yes, you would, Luis. You'd mind if it were Emmett. I'm so glad you're here. If you weren't I'd probably have to spend more time with him. You—" Sensing I was about to say too much, I stopped myself.

Both of us had stretched our arms out when we'd held onto the back of the seats to hoist ourselves up. Now, leaning back on the soft tops of the leather seats, we sat an inch apart from shoulders to wrists. The underside of my forearm was pinkish white next to his tan. Our veins, those miniature inner maps of rivers, ran side by side. Why was it impossible for him to touch me? I looked over at him, but his attention seemed to be elsewhere. The moment had passed. He would say nothing more. Who could I ask about Luis? Who would really know?

A breeze blew in from the water. He slid down in his seat. "Come on. Let's go over to the port. I want to see what's arrived today."

I could have said, "No, I need to get back home." I could have lied about a promise made to Aunt Bertha to do something or go somewhere with her. I didn't. If I had, I might never have seen him again, and I wanted to go on seeing Luis. He had a compelling charm that drew me to him, sexual yet not sexual, an easy acceptance of another person. Emmett had taken to him immediately. Now his jealousy and his stupid prejudice ruined any chance of their friendship. Aunt Bertha was always genuinely pleased to see Luis. Everyone seemed to be. He was usually talking to some stranger when I went to meet him . . . some fisherman, or a tourist, or someone else he'd just met before he broke away to greet me. He worked at a beach house in the afternoons and at night. What were his paintings like? He saw his father some nights. What was he like? His mother had died of cancer three years ago. His brother was killed on Guam. Most of the time he lived in Mexico. Other than these few facts, he was a mystery. Perhaps that was part of his charm also, and he was so different from the boys I'd known. Was I falling in love with Luis? I didn't want to. I wanted relief from the yearning I felt for Tony Gregory, the compulsion to be with him all the time, to hear his voice, to know his body. Every move I'd made, everything I'd done the whole time I was in Colorado was governed by desire. I wanted to avoid that, not to avoid desire entirely but to escape its total rule. Was that possible?

On our way to the docks we passed an old weather-stained house that stood by itself facing the bay. Luis told me some people thought it was Laffite's. There wasn't a bit of red on it, not the slightest tinge.

"I thought he destroyed his house.... Uncle Mowrey said—"

"Yes. People just want to go on believing something's left. Actually he set fire to the whole town. I hope he did it at night."

The reflection of fire in the bay's calm water, smoke rising against a darker sky, ships' sails beginning to unfurl, and on the shore an abandoned dog howling while houses crackled to charred logs—that was what I saw—followed by dawn and wind pushing at smoking piles of ash.

"I wish he had left something."

"I'd rather imagine it than see it. I'd rather imagine Laffite swaggering down to his ship, his men running through the town carrying torches—"

"And the women?"

"On board the ship already, wouldn't they be . . . if they carried any?" He drove on obviously thinking about something far from a pirate village. Restlessness sometimes moved him from one place to another, from one thought to another. I didn't mind; I was often restless myself.

A guard, an old man with a big belly drooping over his belt waved when we stopped at the wharves. "Put it here where I can watch it. Them winos will take anything."

"You think they could carry this little car away?" Luis asked him in Spanish.

The guard grimaced, scratched the back of his neck and answered him rapidly.

I waited beside the car looking at the rows of warehouses wishing they weren't there. I'd expected to see ships right away; instead a long expanse of gray buildings blocked my view. In front of the warehouses ran train tracks, and beyond them stood a deserted granary where pigeons still fluttered from a sagging roost. The granary's gray plastered walls were marked with star shaped pieces of steel rusting in long streaks down its sides. Up near the roof a faded sign read LONE STAR FLOUR MILLS.

"Want to walk down and see the ships?" Luis asked.

"Okay. What did the man say?"

"He wanted to know why I was bringing a beautiful young girl down to this old place."

I looked up at him and laughed. "You lie. Oh, how you lie! He said no such thing. He said he was bored to death with this job, that nothing ever docked here any more but shrimp boats and—"

"I forgot you knew Spanish."

"Not really." I shook my head. I understood more than I could speak and often I barely understood at all.

We moved slowly down the wharf passing doors open to dark warehouses partially filled with bales of cotton and bright orange and white barrels labeled *Paraffin*. Once we'd gotten by all the warehouses I could see an immense freighter. Looking three times as large as the ones out in the bay, the ship floated high above its cargo line. I stopped to touch the taut ropes securing it. Murky brown water reflected scaling metal below the cargo line, and when I stared up, the smokestack was nothing more than a small black cylinder against the sky. Luis wished for a liner because, he said, they were so much more graceful. We walked the length of the freighter. Big as it was, it also looked like a giant toy which, when pushed, would gently float away.

At the end of the wharf we looked out across the bay where other ships waited in dry dock. The narrow end of the bay was lined by the causeway and the railroad bridge Emmett and I had crossed to the island from the mainland. On the opposite side water circled round to the sea.

One other freighter was in port as well along with a coast guard cutter painted a clean gray and stuck with snooty guns pointing high, looking efficient and warlike. A woman in a red and white polka dotted dress chatted with an officer on deck. I glanced up at her face and decided she was too happy to be saying goodbye. Around the corner at another dock we found a line of tugboats with cheerful names like Daisy, Betsy and Sal rocking in their berths.

Walking back to the car I was startled to see Uncle Mowrey standing at the far end of the freighter. From that distance he was so small, a little fat man wrapped in a sagging suit peering up at the mountain of the ship.

Why was he at the wharves? He was usually at his office this time of day. Though I'd never seen it, I thought of the office as a small dark place piled high with dusty ledgers and curling papers. Among them he would bend over rows of tiny figures checking sums, stopping now and then to place faint pencil scratches next to the figures. His sums looked something like the market reports in *The Journal*, indecipherable except to those who knew about the stock market and understood why, for instance, the price of beef was so far down during a drought that was lowering the number of cattle daily.

Except for the brief meetings when he was coming or going from the house or taking one of his short walks to the beach, I had seldom seen him outside. Uncle Mowrey's natural setting was inside, a wall at his back, a newspaper in front of him.

"My uncle—" I gestured toward him.

Luis smiled. "I see him here often."

Intent on the freighter, he didn't notice us. I called to him, and he turned toward us blinking. "Ah." He sighed and bobbed his head in our direction. When he'd shaken Luis's hand he asked, "How's your father?"

"All right. Last night he was winning. Tonight, who knows?"

Mowrey removed his straw hat and wiped the reddened crease on his forehead with a handkerchief. Returning his hat carefully to his head, he lifted his glasses and wiped his eyes. "It's a harmless pastime, Luis."

"I'm afraid it's more than that now."

They talked to each other as if they had met outside a hospital door to discuss the health of a mutual friend who lay just inside helpless in bed.

Mowrey peered out from under his raised glasses. "I'm sorry to hear that."

Stuck in an awkward silence, they stood facing each other. I'd hoped to hear more about Luis's father, so I waited shifting from one foot to the other. Neither one of them could seem to break through the stillness that lay between them like a large invisible boulder. Water lapped at the wharf, metal rigging pieces on the freighters clinked and gulls screamed over an incoming shrimp boat. Finally I asked Uncle Mowrey what he was doing at the wharves.

"It's my pastime, my secret vice. I come down now and then to see what's in port. My father sailed into Galveston Bay on a ship he'd watched being built in Glasgow. Now I come and stand on shore." With one arm he pointed to the warehouses, the decayed buildings, the docks. "I stand here and watch the place rot." He shook his head slightly.

"Come." He waved us over to an open door. "Look in there. What do you see?"

I searched the dark interior of the warehouse behind us. More than half of it was empty. Against the dockside stood bales in orderly rows with metal bindings gleaming faintly against protective burlap covers.

"Cotton," I said.

"That's what made Galveston. Cotton. We had a good natural harbor, one we've made even deeper."

"But you've got cotton still."

"Very little compared to what used to be here. There's the channel to Houston now. People used to say it would never work, no one would want to go that far inland. But they did. Now the trade's gone, has been gone for years. Galveston's hardly a port any more. Now it's the place the whole state runs off to when they want to do what they can't do at home. It's a fine place to raise cain. We've got the medical school and a good hospital, so it's a fine place to be sick. But it's no place to do business. You can go downtown and look at more empty buildings." His voice dwindled away. He looked over at the ship again.

"I planned to get a ship here . . . when I retired, I guess. I wanted to leave from this harbor and to come back here, to come into homeport. I don't know if that will be a possibility. I'll probably have to get in a car and drive over to Houston if I want to go anywhere on a ship." He ducked his head.

I ducked my own. It was embarrassing to hear a quiet man talk so much. It was a little like overhearing something I wasn't supposed to know, and at the same time, I couldn't think of any encouragement I could give him. It was hard to think of something cheerful while standing in the middle of ruin.

"Don't ships still leave from here?" Aunt Bertha, in need of a traveling companion, had taken Mother on a cruise to Cuba in the twenties. She still spoke of dancing with the ship's officers on moonlit decks. The trip had made her a hopeless romantic about traveling anywhere by sea. If she'd been there, she would have talked about how much fun catching a freighter bound for a foreign port would be, an idea my father discouraged whenever she voiced it.

Uncle Mowrey smiled faintly and said cruise ships still sailed from Galveston but not often.

"You'll go someday," I promised lamely.

He nodded, took off his glasses, and wiped his forehead again. "Yes . . . I'll go." He turned away from us taking slow, short steps, stopped, then said if I meant to come home for lunch to bring Luis.

He couldn't come. He had to meet his father.

Mowrey went on to his car. We followed at a distance.

"He's sad, isn't he? An old man with a dream."

"I don't know," said Luis. "He's not so terribly old. He's still got his wife, and he can travel. My father won't go anywhere. I've tried to get him to come back to Mexico with me. He refuses to. He's afraid if he dies there, no one will bring him back here and put him beside my mother. That's all he wants, he says, to lie in a grave beside her. While he waits he gambles. It makes no difference to him whether he wins or loses. It's just something for him to do. Last year he sold our house and moved to the hotel, the Galvez. It's close to the Balinese Club. I stay at the beach house. I hate being closed up in a hotel, but it's what my father wants. All he has to do is walk across the street to the club, and when the night is finished, he comes back again. They all know him there. They know his routine, and everybody does exactly as he wants. The maids don't sweep the hall where his room is till after noon. He can't stand the sound of vacuum cleaners. When he goes downstairs to eat, the headwaiter makes sure he gets his favorite waitress, the one that doesn't talk much." He stopped abruptly and stared up at the sky as if he were searching for the exact position of the noonday sun.

"Can't anything be done?"

Luis bent down so close I could see a flicker of pain in his eyes. "Nothing! I hate all the closed doors and dark corridors. He might as well be living in a mortuary. What can I do about it? Nothing! I come to see him. I wait with him a few weeks. I leave. When this month is over I'll leave him again. I can't stay here with him and force another kind of life on him when he wants to die."

His anger washed over me like a sudden wave I hadn't seen rising. I felt like a child crying for the moon, for all the ice cream I wanted, for everything to be all right. Headed toward the car, we'd stopped at the end of the wharf where there was no shade. The warehouse's metal siding reflected heat. A stench of rotting fish and dank water rose in the still air. Sweat ran down our faces, glistened on our necks, wet our backs. Hot, shaken by Luis's insistence on hopelessness, I swayed on my feet. I'd never heard him be so vehement. He sorrowed over the loss of his mother and his brother. He would shake his head over Emmett's failings. But his father's refusal to go on with his life made his voice harsh and his facial muscles harden into a reproving mask.

"Are you okay?" His voice softened.

"I just felt funny for a minute. I didn't mean to— I guess I shouldn't have asked—"

"It's all right. I get . . . I get mad because there's nothing else I can do. That's all."

The guard waved at us from the door of his shack. "Go now," he shouted in Spanish. "Take your girl to a cool place. She's too young and tender to stay out in the sun."

I pulled a beach towel over the hot leather seat. I should have eaten more breakfast. Hunger was making me dizzy. I slid back in the seat watching Luis down shift gears as we rattled across the railroad tracks.

When he dropped me off at the Mclean house I ran up the steps two at a time, slipped quietly around the umbrella stand and through the hall's welcoming darkness. At the door just outside the alcove to the dining room, I peeked in to find Uncle Mowrey, his newspaper already open before him. In another corner Emmett sat glaring at his boots, one heel balanced on the toe of another. Aunt Bertha came in from the kitchen to put plates on. The chandelier tinkled in the door's quick draft.

"My Lord!" A plate rattled on the table as she put it down. "You scared me half to death." She came over to me and stopped short. "Child, your eyes look like two holes burned in a blanket. You've got to watch the sun down here!" She gave me another appraising look. "Come. Take these plates."

When we sat down Emmett pulled out my chair for me, then stepped over to my side, shoved his hands in both pockets and brought them out full of quarters.

"Finally found me a machine that pays off." He grinned, and I imagined him standing in front of slot machines all morning, standing in dark rooms in front of whirling pictures of fruit—apples, oranges, lemons, cherries.

"You got to kick them now and then." He began piling quarters in symmetrical heaps in front of his own plate.

Forgetting my disgust at the rotting fish smell by the wharf,

I speared cold pink shrimp with a fork and dipped them in red sauce.

Uncle Mowrey consulted his pocket watch, snapped the lid of it shut making a tiny final click, sighed and began eating lunch.

It was like that all month. I'd leave the house, learn something appalling, return and it would be as if nothing had happened. Aunt Bertha's serenity could be easily shattered by Emmett's various disasters—as it was the first time he came home drunk from the rodeo—yet whatever the trouble was, it was absorbed, overlooked, or else, soon forgotten. Perhaps it was because Mowrey and Bertha were older than our parents and, at the same time, we had the privileged standing of visitors. Our parents had to worry about our ordinary lives and their future hopes for us while Bertha and Mowrey weren't inclined to discipline in the first place. Aunt Bertha might worry about Emmett, but she hadn't tattled to his parents. In his case, she chose to be indulgent. As for mine, I'd had long lessons in how to act in other people's houses. Manners, I'd been taught, meant accommodating others. There were times I wished I wasn't the one required to suit everybody else. My brother talked back to our father, got in fights at school. He might be punished, yet he was often silently pardoned and so was Emmett, Mr. Trouble himself wearing noisy boots. I watched him, kept quiet, and minded my manners. But I was tired of doing it sometimes. Why did boys get to be the difficult ones?

One afternoon late Emmett told me, "I found myself a little low-stakes game."

I couldn't imagine anybody playing cards all afternoon, mainly, I guess, because I didn't like sitting around in a darkened room fiddling with pieces of cardboard, but when I said so Emmett only gave me a scornful look

"Poker is a damn fine game!"

"Where are you getting the money?"

"I win sometimes, Celia. God damn!" Glancing toward the open kitchen door he lowered his voice and cocked his head in that direction.

I nodded. There was no need to tell Bertha and Mowrey everything.

So far my own rebellions had been the same small ones of the girls I'd grown up with in Leon. We smoked, sometimes we stayed out too late. The girls we knew who'd resisted their parents most got pregnant. We had no intentions of doing the same. At the university I drank. Jane's crying drunk wasn't the first one I'd ever seen. I'd eventually decided drinking night after night was ultimately silly. The results were always the same; I'd have a hangover compounded by nausea and a headache every morning. And I saw what sometimes happened. Patricia, one of my roommates, had a steady boyfriend, Henry Cale, who used to pick us up and take us to class in his car full of beer cans—there were so many of them rolling around on the floor they fell out when the doors opened. He had already flunked out, gone home to his little town in East Texas, gone home to have nothing to do but drink. I hoped his parents were able to help him. When I asked Patricia, she only shook her head and said she didn't know.

"Celia, Henry . . . he's— I tried to get him to cut down some. He's a lost cause if I ever saw one!"

"Can't he be sent somewhere, you know, some place that will—"

"Yes, but he has to want to go." She shook her head again, and in a week, began dating other boys.

Now and then I thought of Henry Cale driving us down the drag with all his empty beer cans clanking. And I wondered still if he ever did quit drinking.

After lunch a few days later I asked Aunt Bertha if she'd seen Luis around Galveston before I'd brought him to the house.

"I knew his mother, Maxine. His older brother, the one who was killed in the war . . . Ricardo, we called him. Ricky . . .

was one of my best students.

"I didn't know you taught."

She lifted a handful of wet silver from the hot water and dropped it quickly on a dishtowel to drain. "I came down here from Mullin to teach school. That's how I got away. I taught the fourth grade. After Mowrey and I married, I quit teaching."

"So . . . Ricky—"

"Everybody knew him. He was a lovely boy. Handsome. Popular. Played football when he got to high school."

"And Luis?"

"I'd quit teaching by the time he came along."

Drying the silver, sliding the wet knives through the towel, I could almost feel evasion in the kitchen. It was as if some kind of ground fog drifted between me and Aunt Bertha.

"Their father— You know him too?"

She let the water out of the sink, then rinsed her hands carefully under the tap. "We all tried to help him after Maxine died, introduced him to other women. He wouldn't have anything to do with anybody except one old friend of hers. This friend of mine, Eleanor Phillips, lived in the Galvez too. Mowrey said I was meddling. I guess I was. I got Eleanor and Alberto together for dinner here. He spent the whole evening talking about Maxine as if she'd come through the door any minute!"

I laughed when she gestured toward the kitchen door.

"Retired men!" She picked up a dry towel to help me with the glasses. "I don't know what I'll do with Mowrey when he retires! Alberto Platon has nothing to keep him busy. He was a cotton factor and had to retire way early. Not enough to do here."

"So ... Luis ... do you know if he has a girl in Galveston?" I finally asked what I'd been hoping to find out.

"I doubt it. He lives in Mexico most of the time, doesn't he?"

The fog I'd almost seen before thickened and billowed between us. I finished polishing glasses and began pushing a towel round and round a plate trying to remember what my father had said about Randy Wells, the guy all the girls in Leon dated and never married. "Something wrong with his hormones." If that was true, it one of the kinder ways of putting it. Most of the words we had—"queer," "fag," "fruit," "fairy," "homo,"—were meant to hurt. Was Bertha trying not to say one of those?

I dropped the plate and made a lot of apologies while standing above it noticing the flower pattern still evident circling its edges. It was old china, everyday stuff, Aunt Bertha said. It had belonged to her mother-in-law. She was glad to get rid of it. Now she had a good excuse to buy some more sooner. I picked up the fragments. The subject was changed. Bertha and Mowrey would take us to the Balinese Club on the weekend, on Saturday night.

"Mother told me about it. She loved going."

"Did Emmett bring a coat and tie?"

"Aunt Earlene packed one I think. He won't like wearing it."

"I know. I'd just like to see him properly dressed once while he's here."

Nothing was mentioned about getting him a haircut. Bertha might tell him to do it. She knew making Emmett go to a barber was beyond me.

Nothing more was said about Luis either. I wasn't sure she knew what I was asking, and I couldn't question her outright. She was agreeable, but she was older, and perhaps she preferred to avoid the problem altogether. I told myself I was being unreasonable. After all Bertha traveled and, for God's sake, she lived in Galveston. She'd spoken of him kindly. There wasn't a hint of disdain in her voice. She'd been truly glad to see him when he came to the house. I still couldn't ask her. There was nothing effeminate about him. There hadn't been anything effeminate about Randy Wells. He'd kissed all the girls, kissed us all goodbye. And what about Emmett? He was the one who'd met Luis first, and he hadn't said anything. The only fault he'd found with Luis was he was half Mexican. "Meskin," that was what he'd said. Half or whole, it was all the same to Emmett.

Chapter Six

Because of you the sun will shine, the moon and stars will say you're mine, forever and never to part. Be-cause of yo-o-u." The voice on the record wailed on while I tried to lead Emmett around the back porch. Against the wall the white wicker chairs sat like a row of fat old ladies interrupted by stands of Boston fern. The straw rug had been rolled up, and at the edge of it Aunt Bertha watched with the portable phonograph at her side.

"Emmett, try to lead." I was tired of the lesson. All morning Aunt Bertha and I had been trying to teach him how to dance.

"If youall will just change that moony record and get some real music, I'll lead you right off this old porch."

While we were in high school I'd seen him two-stepping around in Leon's VFW Club where the men drank whisky from bottles wrapped in paper bags outside and in the honky-tonk-beer-cafe in McGregor, our nearest wet town, where everybody drank beer inside. Since we'd both gone off to college, I hadn't seen him on any kind of dance floor for a while. He was so stiff-legged and draggy now I wondered if he'd taken Doris Lacey dancing anywhere in the past year. I thought nobody forgot how to dance. It was like bicycle riding. Once you knew, you knew. Emmett clumped around as if he'd never known, and his only excuse was he couldn't two-step to *Because of You*. Surely somebody had taught him more than that, if not his mother, then Doris or one of the whole string of girls he'd dated before meeting her.

Aunt Bertha had already told him this was the only halfway new record she had. "It's not going to do you any good to learn how to keep time with something like *Alexander's Ragtime Band*, is it?"

"Could you?" He asked as if he really thought she might get up and show him. He was ready for any excuse to stop.

"Maybe I could and maybe I couldn't. I'd need your Uncle Mowrey, and it wouldn't hurt if I was twenty pounds lighter and ten years younger. The point is you've got to know how to dance to this kind of music. They don't play western songs out at the Balinese Room. I don't know what they teach you up at that cow college, but you ought to learn to dance to civilized music."

"Cow college!" Emmett howled and dropped my hand. "Why do people who don't know anything about A&M—"

Aunt Bertha grinned. "Texas Agricultural and Mechanical. I know that much."

I backed away from him laughing. Though my university was A&M's oldest rival, I knew real loyalty to his school wasn't behind his anger. He certainly wasn't a member of the ROTC corps whose giant marching formation of the school's initials across the field in step behind the band playing the *Aggie War Hymn* brought students and alumni screaming to their feet. Emmett hated uniforms and drills. He went to A&M only because he had to go somewhere. College kept him out of Korea. His mother meant for him to finish. Somehow, just by doing that, she felt he would put aside his cowboy tendencies. Uncle Estes, as far as I could see, neither agreed nor disagreed with this plan. He seemed to be waiting to see what happened. He wasn't in the least like my father who was usually impatient. Estes, my father said, was a good trader.

I asked him what he meant. His opinions about people were important to me although his ways of judging others were sometimes strange. To him one of the boys I'd dated "looked funny out of his eyes." Though he was a nervous boy, I ignored this remark; on the whole my father usually was a fair judge.

"Estes knows what he's doing, knows livestock well, cattle, sheep, horses. He's got a trained eye, learned it from his daddy. And he's a good businessman, doesn't jump into anything too fast, always knows the important things about people he's dealing with. Oh, he can be fooled. We can all be fooled."

Except for knowing about livestock Emmett had none of the other skills, so while waiting for him to grow into them, Aunt Earlene selected suits at Neiman's, had Emmett's dress shirt pockets monogrammed and ordered low cut shoes as well as silk ties for him. They were—anyone could see—the same sort of clothes Uncle Estes wore when he had to go to a wedding or a funeral.

I'd seen Emmett in a suit only once; at dinner on Christmas Day he wore charcoal gray wool flannel and a new pair of black boots, a compromise he'd made with Aunt Earlene. After dinner he'd mumbled something about scratchy britches, changed back to jeans, and charged out of the back door of our house to the pick-up he'd parked in the drive. He could get out of a house quicker than anybody I knew. I envied him that.

Aunt Bertha's offer of the Balinese Club and her insistence on dancing lessons were maneuvers toward getting Emmett into the summer suit his mother had packed for him. The Chandler women put too much faith in clothes, I thought, as well as too much faith in ways college might change people.

Emmett, quickly tired of defending A&M, fell into the nearest chair.

"Because of yo-o-u," the tenor wailed nasally.

"Cut that thing off, can't you, Aunt Bertha?"

Bertha switched off the phonograph.

"Emmett, you said you wanted to learn."

"Well that was before I got started."

I sprawled on the porch swing. My feet hurt even though I'd insisted on Emmett practicing in his socks. The swing rocked with a reassuring creak, a higher note joining the deep locust hum from the yard. Bertha went inside to bring us iced-tea. Emmett, who looked hungover, sat in his chair, one hand loosely covering his eyes. Why did the simplest kind of dancing seem so hard to him? I stared at the porch's blue ceiling. Aunt Bertha's swing creaked rhythmically; a slight breeze stirred the listless ferns while I daydreamed.

In Leon the Baptist dominated school board hadn't allowed dances. My friends and I had to organize our own outside of school. Maybe Emmett acted like he did because he hadn't gone to any of those. I thought of the long afternoons we'd worked hanging spiraled crepe paper from wall to wall and running to the dime store to buy candles for our mothers' card tables in futile attempts to fill the cavernous VFW Hall we'd rented.

Aunt Bertha handed me a glass of iced-tea.

"You're going to spill it down your neck," Emmett warned as I lay back down in the swing.

I pushed a pillow up behind my head.

"Drink up and let's practice some more." Bertha said.

Emmett shook his head, "No ma'am. It's too hot."

Bertha looked at him closely, judging his tolerance. "All right."

Emmett frowned. His dark hair fell in curls over his forehead. Nobody was even trying to make him get a haircut.

"I just hope they play that song tonight," he sighed.

"Which song?" Bertha studied the circles of water on the tray in her lap.

"*Because of You.*"

"You can always request it." Bertha smeared the water over the tray with a paper napkin, put it down on the nearest table, and walked into the house. We could hear her turn and go upstairs.

She was abrupt like that at times. Perhaps she was tired of both of us, or just tired of trying to make Emmett act right. She would, when her patience wore thin, or when she felt enough time had been spent in argument, simply walk away from a disagreement. This made Emmett furious. In his family, he was the one who stalked off leaving people fuming. Today, however, he ignored Aunt Bertha's exit.

He eased out of his chair and came over to the swing. Pushing my legs over, he sat down.

"You were late getting in last night," I said.

"Yeah."

"How's Jane?"

"Okay."

"I thought maybe she and Rob—" I was trying not to say too much about her. I'd seen so little of him the past few days I didn't know if he was still interested in her or not. I hoped he was. If he was busy chasing Jane, I could continue to see Luis without interference.

"They just go around in the summer when they're both home. They all go out with each other. Rob brought Leslie last night."

"And Marion?"

"Gone to Canada, thank God, with his family. We went to a couple of clubs."

"Anybody ask for ID?"

"In Galveston?"

"Okay! Okay!"

"She drinks too much." Emmett stared out over the back yard in the direction of the magenta oleanders.

"Jane? I thought you were the one who did that."

"I'm not an alky. Once she gets started, she won't stop. I have to take her home just before she passes out."

"I'm impressed."

"Goddamn, Celia, don't be sarcastic."

"Emmett! It's just— It's funny, you looking after somebody else."

"I don't know about that. Drunks aren't any fun, are they?" He laughed. "This is a hell of a vacation. Here I am running around with an alky and you with a spic."

He didn't really know anything about Luis. Why would he? Luis was older, and he was— What was he?

Sometimes Luis painted late at night, working against the dark, he said. I'd been to his studio, the living room of a small house way down on West beach. Perched on stilts, wind battered, stained gray by salt air, it looked like it might be carried away by the slightest wind. Inside during the day, light poured through windows overlooking the Gulf. Lack of north light apparently didn't concern him. The studio was crammed with things. There were jars and boxes full of paint tubes, seashells, an old white kitchen table covered with splotches of paint, topographical maps of the Galveston quadrant of Texas, and maps of Mexico City rolled into tubes stuck in an old crate hanging on the wall. Over it hung his mother's Panama straw beach hat. An empty luggage rack was propped against the same wall next to a bookcase full of skeletons of fish heads, bones—cows' I guessed—masks he'd brought from Mexico, stones and a row of rusty metal cans of all sizes that had washed up on the beach. Somehow these looked far more interesting in an awkward line with every dent showing than they might have looked on the beach. Above the clutter or sometimes tucked within it, were pictures, old photographs of his parents and his brother Rico.

It was all random and hodgepodge. He had to have a lot of things, he said, a lot of angles to catch the light. All of it was used—in a way I couldn't actually understand—in his work. Perhaps the things he'd collected from the world around him curled, pushed, sometimes shattered and fell into his pictures combined with a vision he had, or one he made up as he went along, something he didn't know he had until he saw it on canvas. I wondered aloud about what he called the work he was doing.

"Abstract expressionism maybe. Call it that if you want. Most people have to call it something, have to have names for things."

"Does that bother you?" I asked.

"Not really. I'd go on painting no matter what it's called. One of my teachers, the best one, was an expressionist. I'm still, I guess, trying to paint my way away from him, away from his way of looking. He taught me a lot. Now I have to teach myself."

Was he at the beach house now stubbornly staring at a canvas, trying to see something, trying to make something?

He'd told me though he always sketched a lot, he never tried to mirror an object when he painted. At times I wondered if he painted partially to push reality out of his head. He might be sitting on the porch staring out to sea, or could he be with his father somewhere else? I didn't think so, but it was impossible to know, to even imagine how he lived through a whole day as much as I might try.

I used to get Tony Gregory to describe his days in great detail, so I could visualize him in the shower, in his apartment eating breakfast, in class or the library, talking to another student. I had literally memorized his schedule. I wanted to be able to remind myself, "He's eating lunch now. He's on his way to that class on contracts. After that he'll probably go to the library." Where was he on his way to now? Who was walking through the day with him? Where would he be that evening?

Determined not to think of him, I picked up a book, put it down, and called Leslie.

The Jamaican was sitting on the steps in front of the pier when I got to the seawall. Beside him was his drum. Leslie was nowhere in sight.

"I heard you drumming the other night."

He looked up. "I didn't see you."

"It was late. We just drove by. I was with some people."

"Come early next time." He looked away, seemed to draw into himself, to wish, perhaps, I'd leave. A line of conch shells in the shop window above his head gaped like open mouths.

"Would you . . . ? Please tell me your name."

"I got a lot of names. Here they call me Tom-Tom." He finally smiled.

"I've heard. What do they call you other places?"

"Depends . . . depends on who's doing the calling and what place."

"Jamaica. What did they call you in Jamaica?"

"Cal. My friends call me Cal."

"I'm Celia."

"Celia. Your mother name you that?"

"It was her first name. Everybody called her by her middle name, so she gave me her first one."

"You the first born?"

"Yes."

Across the street Leslie got out of a car. She waved. The wind blew her dark hair away from her face. Like mine, her hair was cut short except hers curled. The damp air only made it curl more. She had on white shorts and a white shirt neatly tucked in which made her look tidy even when she was windblown.

Later, wading in the surf with her after lunch, I mentioned Tom-Tom.

"He's here every summer lately."

"Luis says he has some family here."

"Maybe. I don't know. Living here you get used to people just showing up. And, except for going off to UT, I've always lived on the island."

Luis hadn't . . . he lived there, or in Guanajuato, or in other parts of Mexico, I supposed. I wanted to ask Leslie about him, but asking was awkward. I didn't know her well. Perhaps she'd be embarrassed by the question. We went to the same university; so did thousands of others. Watching the small waves nibbling at the sand, I fretted inwardly. She was the only person in Galveston I could think to ask, and now that she was here, I couldn't make myself say anything. I liked her though I hardly knew her. I'd liked her when we first met. Despite the nervous laugh, she was smart and quick. She told me she'd planned to be a counselor at a girls' camp that summer. Her mother was ill in June, so she'd stayed home. Now, at the last part of the summer, she felt she was only wasting time.

"Mother's fine now. I run around with Rob and Marion and Jane because I've known them always. There's nothing else left to do till school starts. I'm sick of Galveston. Next summer I'm going to Europe. I've got to get out of here."

"Funny, isn't it? I had to get out of Leon, so here I am in Galveston."

We laughed at each other, at ourselves.

She was working on a degree in art history.

"I'll need an advanced degree before I can do anything much with it. Right now...this fall I've got a part time job with an architectural historian . . . looking up stuff in the library. Actually I'm pretty good at it." She laughed. "I like finding out about obscure things . . . how many new chairs Thomas Jefferson ordered for Monticello, what plumbing was like in the early 1900s."

Her nervous laugh had disappeared. Now she simply smiled.

"That's my job too, or part of it. I'll be working at *The Texan* again. I won't be paid though. Only the editors get paid."

"I'm really an assistant to the assistant who's a grad student. And I can't make enough to go to Europe on. My parents will help, they say. It won't exactly be the grand tour. I'll use trains and I'll bike as much as I can."

Two other girls I knew in journalism school thought they might work as reporters or go into advertising if they didn't marry first. Some other friends majored in elementary education, but all of them planned to marry as soon as possible. Leslie was the first girl I'd met who seemed to want to do anything but marry the minute she graduated.

"Maybe I'd like to do that . . . to go to Europe."

"On a bicycle?"

"It sounds like fun." We waded in the surf, sandals in hand. Later that afternoon, our mouths reddened from licking strawberry snow cones, we sat under an umbrella talking, and I found I could ask about Luis.

"Oh God!" Leslie said. "I didn't know you knew him. Everybody wonders. I mean . . . it's possible, but I don't know, not really. He's living in Mexico now, isn't he?"

"Most of the time."

"It would be hard to be a queer down there, wouldn't it? I mean macho is it in Mexico. Maybe—" She gave me a long, questioning look. "Maybe he's both ways."

"Oh, come on!"

"No. I mean it. Some guys are. They like men and women."

"How do you know?"

"My brother. He's older. He's told me about— About guys like that."

"Are there many?

"I don't know." She looked out to the water then turned back to me. "I don't guess you could find out in an interview."

Leslie leaned back, laughing outright, and I laughed with her hoping she hadn't noticed my light-hearted reaction was a little forced. My naiveté continually embarrassed and astonished me. I would have been glad for an older brother, glad for someone to tell me things. Kenyon never told me anything. He was far too busy getting in and out of trouble, barely making his grades in high school and going away to military school afterward. I knew it was the wrong choice, but he'd had a friend who promised he was going too, then didn't. He came home miserable and kept coming until he was AWOL most of the time. Of course our father had liked the idea of him going. He had an almost religious belief in the ability of the army to shape up young men, and he didn't understand Kenyon. None of us did. At times it seemed I knew so little about anything that I moved through the days managing in a half-knowing way, questioning as I went, but sometimes not even knowing I should question. I had only a wisp of knowledge about homosexuality, the one remark the colonel had made about hormones.

Mother never mentioned any other sexual possibilities. All her instructions concerned the possibility of pregnancy, and everyone else's mother in Leon was the same. It was a wonder, I decided, that any of the girls I'd grown up with were interested in sex at all. Tony Gregory said all the warnings, all the secrecy, all the repetition of "nice girls don't" only made us more interested. I'd laughed at him, then agreed. The forbidden enticed. I was fearful of what I'd find out; at the same time I was determined to know. Was that why I was so curious about Luis? Everybody wonders, Leslie had said.

"Listen, have you ever—" I made little circles in the sand with one finger. "In the library. Have you ever looked it up?"

She looked out at the ocean again and shook her head slightly. "Not here . . . not in the school library. When could you? I mean . . . you wouldn't have wanted anybody— Oh, they didn't have that kind of information in our high school library! Or if they did, we never could find it. At the university there's plenty. They've got Freud and Ellis, stuff like that, but what can you really learn about sex in books?"

She sounded so sophisticated I was embarrassed all over again, so embarrassed I was half-angry at Leslie, half-angry at myself because of my ignorance. I insisted, "Something. You found out something! Anything would be better than total stupidity. Better for me anyway. I've got a brother, but he's too much younger to tell me anything, and he probably wouldn't if he knew."

"What about Emmett? Doesn't he—"

"The king of the cowboys? Oh, he only knows the usual stuff—men and women. He knows the words for the others . . . probably what they do, or some of it. He doesn't like Luis anyway. Boys like Emmett—" I shrugged. "He hardly wants to be believe it's 1953. He wants to think it's 1880, and he just rode into town to hit the whorehouses and saloons."

"I know. He got Rob to take him over to Post Office Street."

"Did he?"

"Yeah. The other night . . . after the rodeo."

I started to tell her I thought he'd been with Jane and caught myself. Leslie was Jane's friend, one of her oldest friends. Obviously Emmett hadn't been there all night. I wondered how Post Office Street was different from Nuevo Laredo, but I wasn't about to ask him.

We were all dressing in the big upstairs bedrooms. Aunt Bertha, whose collecting passions seemed to ebb and surge like tides, had at one time been struck by the desire for Victorian dressers; the three she'd bought had been stationed, one on her side of the room, two on our side. I'd used the mirror over the sink in the bathroom to put on make-up. It felt funny, like a tight mask on top of my tan, but there wasn't time to wash it off. We'd had to take turns getting dressed in there. Now I had trouble seeing if my slip was showing in my dresser's high mirror. I looked up to catch Emmett, his back to me, frowning at a spot of dried blood on his chin. Uncle Mowrey, over on his side, stood engrossed in the problem of spacing thinning hair over his scalp while sharing his dresser with Aunt Bertha who screwed and unscrewed tops of a collection of small bottles on the marble top and muttered about her make-up. We could have been mother, father, brother and sister, a family like my own, though my own never finished dressing in a room together. Mother might come to my doorway, or I might walk through Kenyon's room, but whenever we wanted, we stayed in our own rooms and shut our doors. Here that privacy was impossible.

I backed further away from the mirror and still couldn't see the hem of my skirt.

"Is my slip showing?"

"Just a minute," said Emmett. He and Uncle Mowrey had begun tying their ties. Both of them leaned toward the center of their mirrors, Mowrey threading his tie through the knot efficiently, Emmett struggling with his like a man who'd decided to hang himself and be done with it.

Aunt Bertha kept dabbing on lipstick with one finger. Every time she missed the outline of her lips she used another tissue.

"Why don't you go downstairs, Celia, and look at yourself in that full length mirror in the living room?" She crumpled another tissue in her hand and let it fall on the small withered pile in front of her.

After avoiding that mirror since the first day I'd been there, I had no intention of running downstairs to use it. The distortion I knew I'd find would spook me again.

"It isn't true," I said.

"It's true enough to see whether a petticoat is showing or not."

Emmett turned around. "It isn't showing."

I put my hands over my eyes. "Aggh!"

"What's wrong with you, Celia?"

"You can't wear that tie!" I peeped out at him between crossed fingers.

"Why not? It's a perfectly good tie!"

"It's perfectly hideous!"

Uncle Mowrey looked up from the coat he was brushing and Bertha, clutching her glasses in one hand, twisted around to see. We all waited until she put her glasses on and lifted them higher up on her nose.

"Lord!"

The tie, much wider than anyone wore, was a painted monster with a covered wagon and horses roaring down its full length. A cloud of yellow dust followed two brown horses and a bright red wagon. Green prickly pear grew on either side of the yellow and brown road.

Uncle Mowrey cleared his throat but said nothing.

Aunt Bertha said, "It's . . . it's a little active."

I went to the corner closet to search for the tie Aunt Earlene must have selected for him to wear with his new navy suit.

"You won't find it." Emmett waited behind me. "Mother forgot to pack my tie, I guess. I bought this one this morning."

"Why don't you borrow one of Uncle Mowrey's?" I whispered.

"I'm not going to borrow anybody's tie. If I've got to wear one, it's going to be one of my own."

I pushed the closet door shut. "All right. Wear it then. I hope you choke on it."

"You children!" said Aunt Bertha.

We walked over to her part of the room, Emmett looking correct and sober, his tie splotched on his white shirt. My cheeks were flushed, and my hair fell wildly over my forehead. I ran my fingers through it.

Bertha handed me a brush. "Here." She smiled. "Luis might be there. His father gambles at the Balinese often."

Emmett, obviously pretending not to hear, stared at the ceiling.

"All right then. Let's go." Aunt Bertha led the way.

A parade. That's what we were, the fat lady first followed by clowns. Oh, look at the one with the funny tie. Oh, look at the one with the funny hair. And there's the ringmaster following. Uncle Mowrey, holding the rolled newspaper he'd been reading while Emmett and I quarreled, tapped the banister with it as we marched downstairs.

I was wearing the first dress and high heels I'd had on since arriving in Galveston and felt hampered by so many clothes. My slip clung to me. Stockings and garter belt encased all my lower body, and in place of the knotted shirt I usually wore, a belt was tightly buckled around my waist. My dress outlined my breasts; a necklace coiled around my neck. I would have gladly kicked off the shoes and ripped the binding layers of clothes away. Everything scratched, slid, irritated. I thought longingly of the pleasures of nakedness, of women who tied a piece of cotton around their hips and sauntered barefoot on island sands . . . islands far away where no one wore make-up and where no nightclubs existed. Surely there was an island left somewhere without a nightclub. I'd looked forward to going to the Balinese Room. Now I didn't want to go at all, not even to see Luis.

Getting all dressed up to walk to a nightclub decorated as if it were some place in the South Seas when it was on the end of a pier in Galveston was silly. Piers were for fishing or looking at the ocean. They had their uses. Nightclubs . . . I thought of the ones we went to in Austin. On the other side of town across the river was the Tower, nothing more than a tall white stucco covered form sticking up like an awkward thumb over the entrance. Inside a huge mirrored ball revolved over the middle of the dance floor all night, and everyone said if you were drunk, you began to revolve too. Or, out by the lake, which was too small for yachts, there was Yacht Harbor where we danced outside every spring on a floor outlined with multi-colored lights reflected in the dark water. The New Orleans, closer to the university, was a series of small candlelit rooms filled with wrought iron tables and chairs, but there was no jazz. A jukebox, yellow, red, and green, bubbled at the edge of the dance floor as one did every place we went. I didn't want to drink and dance any place that night, not with Emmett, not with anyone.

Just ahead of me Emmett ran one finger between his neck and the back of his shirt collar. No wonder he hated suits. No wonder he hated ties and shoes that laced and coats that had to be buttoned. Wouldn't he be happier in a breechcloth? But there was so much of him, and a breechcloth would cover so little. . . .

"What are you giggling about?" Emmett looked over at me. We were waiting with Aunt Bertha for Uncle Mowrey to back the car out of the garage. Though I had on my highest heels, he was still a head taller.

"Nothing."

I glanced up past him to the sky, which held the sun's afterglow. The rotting sweet smell of oleanders hung in the air. No breeze lifted the branches. Nothing fluttered, moved, stirred. There was often this dead calm at sunset as if the day had given up. It made me even more restless and a little sad.

Uncle Mowrey backed his bulky Olds out of the garage. For a moment, hearing the engine's stutter in the stillness, I detested all mechanical noises. I wanted the world to stay quiet, to wait with me for the sun to go down.

Emmett opened the back door for me. Tonight we were the children, substitutes perhaps, for those Aunt Bertha and Uncle Mowrey never had. Did the same thought occur to them? They must have wanted children at one time. I stooped to climb in the car and hit my head against the frame.

"Damn!"

My necklace felt as if it were strangling me. I bent my head and fumbled with the catch.

Emmett slid down in the seat next to me and unfastened the necklace. His fingers brushed my neck.

"Don't!" I said feeling an involuntary chill arise.

"Why not?" he whispered, then seeing Aunt Bertha's eyes on us in the rearview mirror, he lifted his head.

"There." He gave me an appraising look. "You don't really need it" With one hand he stuffed the necklace in his coat pocket. His other hand still rested on the back of my neck as if he'd decided, once more, to claim me.

I twisted away from him suddenly thankful for the layers of clothes I'd put on. Emmett could make me feel almost naked.

Chapter Seven

There was a family, just one, the Maceos, who were in charge of liquor by the drink and gambling in Galveston. Uncle Mowrey insisted everybody knew them, knew what they did. Of course, he granted, their business was illegal, but the family ruled carefully. There were no gang wars; there were few deaths. The family gave a lot of money to charity. Most of all, tourists continued to come to the island, to stay in the hotels, to eat in the restaurants and to enjoy what Uncle Mowrey and Aunt Bertha clearly considered minor vices. It was better for people who needed a vacation from the thou-shalt-nots to come to Galveston, lose a little money playing cards or the slots, and drink a few mixed drinks than it was to remain at home with nothing but more scoldings.

On the way to the Balinese Room, Aunt Bertha told us how the Texas Rangers raided it. "They run out here in plain-clothes, and by the time they get to the door—before then actu-ally—they know they're coming. Someone always tattles. Every bellboy in town knows when the Rangers arrive."

We were walking down a long private pier where anyone could walk, but only those who paid their dues could walk through the locked door at the end. A dark green marquee covered us, its canvas sides and roof, strung taut; it was buffeted by continual winds. Below us waves curled and crashed around the pilings throwing spray high into the air though never high enough to reach the walkway.

"By the time they're inside those doors—" She stopped to gesture toward the double glass doors at the far end of the green tunnel. "When they get there, the roulette tables are hidden in the walls like folding beds. At least one is left one out. It's cov-ered with a green felt top, and all the dealers are shooting pool on it just as the Rangers come in."

"They've never been caught?" Emmett asked.

"No, I don't think so. Not while people are playing. You have to go through a lot of other doors to get to those tables." She pulled her shawl up over her shoulders. "Sometimes they close it down for a while. I suppose the Rangers have to win every now and then." She said this is such a determined manner I suspected she'd never been there when the place was raided. Aunt Bertha was only repeating a story she'd been told. Probably the Rangers hadn't been that gullible, nor had the dealers been such obvious play actors, but it was a story that Galveston people liked to tell if they, like Aunt Bertha, thought that tourists wanted relief from thundering preachers and tight-lipped elders.

One of the two men at the front door welcomed my aunt and uncle calling them by name.

Mowrey answered, "Evening, Frank." His tone was such that I knew he'd grown accustomed to saying just that and not a word more to this particular man.

We were led down a long stretch of carpet printed with enormous swirling leaves to a room glittering with mirrors between murals. For a moment we stood across from one showing a Balinese looking woman balancing a bowl of fruit on her head. On her island in front of unreal mountains there were palms that were too green without a single ratty looking brown leaf like all those we saw every day in Galveston. A gleaming, almost phosphorescent light, hidden in the ceiling, played over people's heads. Frank faded behind us to be replaced by a similar man with grayer hair. His white tux shirt glowed in the light. We were led around tables and rattan chairs to a deep booth near a small parquet floor where people were already dancing. Four huge fake palm trees, blue-green fronds drooping, sprouted from each of the dance floor's corners. Against the back wall a small band played on the stage, but all I could see, at first, was a gleaming jumble of brass instruments, mirrors, and more murals. I kept searching for windows then realized there were none. Menus nearly the size of a tabloid newspaper, copies of the one I'd already seen with the stylized Polynesian girl's face, were passed to us. I held mine in front of me like a shield.

Why, I wondered, were restaurants always pretending to be some place else? Why couldn't this one simply be in Galveston? Here, years after the war's long bloody campaign when we'd fought for island after tiny island, the music of Broadway's *South Pacific* had conquered. The dream of that remote, beautiful place had been imitated by interior decorators, readily accepted by the owners, and displayed to the public so people could pay for the dream and pretend to have been magically transported to a far greener, far more opulent island. I couldn't understand the necessity of this transformation and I hated the pretense. San Francisco with its bays and bridges and wharves was San Francisco. Why couldn't Galveston be Galveston? In the hotel, in the Galvez, it was, but here we were all supposed to be in Bali. Wasn't this island exotic enough?

Uncle Mowrey ordered a round of Tom Collins for us all. The pages of the menu, offering an elaborate mixture of Italian and Chinese food, yawned before me. I chose redfish. Emmett ordered sirloin well done. He said he always ordered steak when he ate out; it was the least he could do for the cattle market. Trapped by the long drought, ranchers had to sell low. Emmett's appetite could do nothing for starving cows on dried out pastures, and he knew it. He was only saying something his father probably said.

His and Aunt Bertha's voices floated above my head. I kept listening for the sound of waves that I couldn't seem to hear. The great crash and wash of water was submerged by air-conditioning, hidden under the languid music oozing around the wall, the rattle of cutlery, and clamor of people's voices.

Emmett, who had been scanning the room also, finally asked, "Where's the roulette?"

"Through those doors. Right over there." Bertha nodded toward mirrored doors across from us. "They play craps too."

I looked over at Uncle Mowrey. "Do you play?"

He shook his head and smiled. "I watch Bertha. She plays for jewelry."

"He stakes me," she said. Her diamond rings twinkled as she touched Uncle Mowrey's hand. She wore a small constellation that night; beside the rings she had on two diamond bracelets and a pin and earrings equally glittering.

Mowrey laughed. He didn't look embarrassed; he was merely amused. Much of what she did seemed to amuse him in the same way my mother's cursing tickled my father. She didn't do it often, but when she did, he grinned and shook his head as if to say he didn't know what she'd do next.

Uncle Mowrey looked at his wife like that now, as if he was both proud and confounded by something she'd done.

"So far," Aunt Bertha said, "I've won this pair of earrings and a diamond bar pin."

"So you're lucky?"

"Sometimes I lose."

Uncle Mowrey smiled. "She doesn't count the losses."

I glanced away from them to see Luis and a middle-aged man with heavy half-circles under his eyes standing nearby. Mr. Platon's gaze drifted generally over the room. Luis talked to someone just behind them. As he turned back toward his father, he saw me and came over, urging his father to walk slightly in front of him. The older man moved slowly through the rattan chairs as if he didn't care where he was going, as if his son's will was all that propelled him.

"Here comes that Meskin," said Emmett. "Looks like he's got another one with him."

"Hush!" Bertha said.

At the same time I whispered, "Quit being an idiot!"

Uncle Mowrey stood up, the edge of his coat nearly meeting the table's rim. "My niece," he said, "my nephew," and repeated our names to Mr. Platon.

He shook hands with Uncle Mowrey and nodded briefly in our direction. Did he see us? Or had he just nodded out of long habit?

"You're looking well," Bertha chirped.

Emmett began drawing lines in the tablecloth, digging into it with a table knife. At the same time he held his back straight against the back of the booth like an angry animal forced to retreat.

Mr. Platon stared down at Aunt Bertha. His eyelids flickered. He seemed to withdraw like an immense old turtle retreating into his shell.

"Won't you join us?" Uncle Mowrey asked.

"Thank you. We've already eaten." His tone remained polite though he was answering from a distance.

"My father and I are—" Luis began.

"Yes, we are just on our way." Mr. Platon nodded toward the back of the room. "I must see how my luck runs tonight." He moved away as automatically as he'd moved toward us.

Luis hesitated. "Celia, save me a dance?" For the first time he smiled.

I nodded, and he followed his father.

Emmett studied Aunt Bertha's and Uncle Mowrey's faces carefully searching for their reactions. "What's the matter with him?" There was a scornful edge to his voice.

Bertha explained. "He's . . . He's mourning his wife. She's been dead for several years, but—" She looked down at the table as if she might find an explanation hiding somewhere in the silver or in the cocktail glasses. "And he's a gambler. He can't stop that either. He comes out here nearly every night."

"What does he play? Craps?"

"No. Roulette."

"Does he win?"

"No one wins every night, Emmett. It doesn't seem to make Alberto much difference though. He just keeps on. He must have run through a fortune, or else he's got some sort of system."

Uncle Mowrey shushed her. Mention of somebody else's money made him uncomfortable. He refused to answer Emmett's questions about "Old Platon's fortune." His professional discretion, the absolute refusal to discuss other people's finances, was obviously his life's rule, and Aunt Bertha obviously respected his silence on the subject. He made their living keeping his mouth shut.

Emmett didn't care. That was his way, to blunder through difficult questions, to ignore others' quirks and habits. And he was worse at the moment because he had just one objective that evening. The Balinese was the only private club he was liable to get into in Galveston. He'd already played the slots until he didn't have a nickel left in his pockets some days, and he'd played in small stakes poker games hidden in little rooms in bars all over town. This was his one chance to try roulette. He'd set aside—he'd told me—two, maybe three hundred dollars for that particular evening. Obviously he was determined to play. Sometimes I wondered if he'd ever stop, if he'd become as addicted to gambling as Luis's father seemed to be.

While we were waiting for supper, Uncle Mowrey and Aunt Bertha showed us the room where people played roulette. Strangely the light was brighter in there as if the glowing darkness surrounding us in the dining room had given way. The light, I felt, announced the primary reason for the club's existence; gambling was serious here. Mr. Platon was standing by one of the tables with some others watching the wheel whirl, watching the little white ball clatter and spin and fall into one of the colored slots. Black and red, black and red alternated from one to thirty-six. On opposite sides there were two green slots marked zero and double zero, and behind the wheels stood men in tuxedos, related by birth, disposition, or interest to Frank, the keeper of the front door. Was it merely the tuxes they all wore, or did they all truly resemble each other? Was there a family nose, a set of ears, a chin? I examined them closely but couldn't discern a likeness except they all seemed reserved; they withheld themselves repeating, at the door and dining room, the usual greetings. At the roulette tables they only announced the beginning of the game and the winning numbers. All of them were watching us. It made me a little dizzy to watch the wheel; instead I studied the players putting chips on numbers and colors on either side of them. There were numbers in some of Luis's pictures . . . huge nines and fives repeated in red and in black on white as if his father's addiction had seeped through to him. Why shouldn't it have? Why shouldn't he worry about a fortune disappearing? Yet he'd never mentioned it. He didn't attempt to stop his father. Perhaps he couldn't. Perhaps he didn't care about the money. Emmett would have cared. So would have Kenyon. He'd take any kind of job to avoid being broke. My own father would have cared, and I guessed, Uncle Mowrey would have too.

We urged Emmett away from the roulette wheels and returned to the dining room. Aunt Bertha suggested that after all those lessons we really should dance.

It was a tiny crowded floor, but I could follow Emmett. He moved easily and naturally with the music as if he'd never had a lesson in his life and didn't need one.

"What kind of act were you putting on?"

"When?"

"You know when! Aunt Bertha and I were trying to teach you how to dance, and you acted like you didn't know. You could hardly drag yourself around the floor."

"I don't know how when people are watching me."

"People are watching you now! All those people in the booths, Aunt Bertha, Uncle Mowrey—" I waved to them as we went past.

"They aren't telling me how. Nobody's saying put this foot here and that foot there."

He stopped in the middle of the floor and did a jerky imitation of the pattern we'd tried to teach him. "Besides I forget what I'm doing when I'm dancing with you out here." He gathered me to him and moved back into the crowd.

I tried to pull away from him slightly, to keep a little space between us. It seemed ridiculous for him to insist on this intimacy when none actually existed between us, not even the casual, everyday intimacy of friendship.

His arm tightened around me.

"Let go!" I whispered.

"No."

I couldn't see his face, but I was sure he was laughing.

Luis, walking through the other dancers, said hello to two or three people on his way toward us.

"Here comes your spic."

"Will you quit being so stupid!"

Luis tapped Emmett's shoulder, but he ignored him.

"Let me dance with Luis, Emmett."

"No."

"If you won't, I'm going to scream." I said quietly. I hadn't known . . . hadn't planned on what I might do.

"Here?"

"Here!" I almost shouted.

"All right." His voice grated. He let go of me so suddenly I had to steady myself against Luis. Turning away from us, he brushed into another couple, excused himself and swaggered off the floor toward the roulette room.

Luis looked down at me, took my hand, and put his arm around me leaving just the amount of space I'd tried to keep between myself and Emmett. He was a good dancer, better than Emmett. We moved around the floor so naturally it seemed we had been dancing together for years. Except for the day we sat on top of the seats talking about his brother, this was as close as I'd ever been to Luis. Now he was holding me, and for the first time, we were touching each other. I wanted that closeness to go on and on. Parted from the struggle with Emmett, held lightly, I was blissfully free for a moment.

Then the combo changed from playing a jazzy version of *Ruby* to *Among My Souvenirs*, a song I'd liked when I was dating Tony Gregory and hated now. *Some letters tied with blue. A photograph or two. I see a rose from you among my souvenirs.* I had the letters. He'd sent me a picture of himself. There were no roses. When I was with him the song seemed to be about someone else's nostalgia, but once we'd parted, it was nothing but a long aching sigh of my own longing. Hearing it, I was filled with self-loathing. I didn't want to be sentimental about Tony. I thought I should let him go, yet longing, I was discovering, couldn't be easily governed. I wished I'd had more time with him. It seemed Tony, like Emmett, just wanted a girl, not me specifically. I must have talked myself into thinking he loved me since my place was so quickly taken once I was gone.

Luis was saying something. I'd been so lost in the music I could hardly hear him. He was asking something. What was it?

"Your cousin—?"

"Emmett's jealous, I guess. He doesn't want me to be with anyone else." What else could I say? How could I explain his abruptness? I couldn't tell Luis, "My cousin doesn't like you because you're part Mexican. And I'm . . . I'm not even sure you like girls!" The falsity of everything hit me . . . dancing with him while longing for Tony, trying to deny Tony, utterly denying Emmett.

We'd danced to the far edge of the floor. I couldn't see Bertha and Mowrey. I thought the night would never be over, that I'd spend hours dancing with Luis who was now lost in his own silence. In the hours to come, I would have to dutifully eat my supper while chatting with Aunt Bertha and Uncle Mowrey. After that we'd all probably go watch Emmett play roulette. That I was there at all dancing on the edge of a floor suspended over the waves I could neither see nor hear was too unreal. Aunt Bertha and Uncle Mowrey had been so determined to show us a good time. I detested every minute of it and detested myself as well for being ungrateful.

If I could have seen Bertha and Mowrey, would I have acted as I did? Would their presence, the continual sight of two middle-aged married people have anchored me somehow? I doubted it. At that point they were only people I liked well enough. And if my parents had been sitting there instead of the Mcleans, perhaps they wouldn't have mattered much either. I had to be free of the lot of them, free of all demands, free of Emmett, of Luis, of Tony. The entrance to the corridor was across the room. Threading my way through the other dancers, past the gray-haired *maitre de*, I ran almost silently over the carpet's swirling leaves down the long hall to the double glass doors where the man Uncle Mowrey had called Frank stood staring at me.

"Celia! Wait!" Luis called. He was somewhere in the hall behind me.

Frank raised his eyebrows slightly as though asking me silently if he should open the door or not.

I couldn't wait on Frank. I pushed the door open myself and looked down the long canvas-covered tunnel where lights had been turned on inside. At the far end there was nothing but darkness.

"Where are you going?" Luis was beside me.

"I don't know. I hate this place!"

I started walking down the pier and almost fell when one of my heels got stuck in a crack between the planks. Balancing myself by holding onto his arm, I took off my shoes and carried them, one in either hand.

"Your aunt and uncle— Won't they be worried?"

"I can't help that either."

We were at the end of the marquee. A fresh wind billowed round my skirt. I kept walking to shore. On either side I could see black waves rising and falling leaving a white line of foam lit by the city's lights on the seawall.

Pausing for only a minute, we stepped off the pier then ran through traffic veering right to the opposite side of the wide boulevard, lined at this point, with souvenir shops, a motel and little clubs. Their neon signs, *88 KEYS, TWIN PALMS, THE PIRATE'S DEN*, glittered and blinked yellow, red, green in the night.

Immediately in front of us was the small carnival we never went to. A double line of bulbs arced over the entrance to it. I stared toward those. One bulb was burned out. At the far end of the carnival's grounds I could see a roller coaster outlined by lights writhing against the sky. Keeping my eyes on its highest curve, I started wandering toward it conscious of the gritty sand and pebbles under my stockinged feet. Far down the midway over the heads of the crowd, the coaster's cars sped up and down its looping curves. Around me a babble of voices rose and fell like the murmuring sea.

"Where are you going?" Luis was still beside me.

"I don't know. I had to get out of there. I . . . I couldn't stand it." I bumped into someone.

"Well, pardon you!"

A skinny old lady eating ice-cream out of a pint carton. Chocolate. I stared at the green plastic spoon resting in the carton. She'd eaten almost the whole pint.

"I was on my way over to them slot machines." She pointed with the spoon toward a row of machines lining the walls of an open booth. Someone was in front of every one of them. I half expected to see Emmett's back, his familiar height, his slack stance.

The old lady licked the spoon meditatively and stared at me as if she meant to continue, and I was the only barrier in her path.

I brushed blindly past her and ducked into an open door.

"Hey!" A man's voice shouting. "Hey, you can't go in there!"

I had nothing with me, no purse, no billfold. I looked around to see Luis paying the barker. A violent burst of wind blew my skirt up. There was another doorway. I ran through it to mirrors—a wall of mirrors reflecting thin, fat, elongated, squeezed up, bent, stretched, totally distorted versions of myself crying, a shoe dangling from either hand. I dropped my shoes.

"Celia, come out," Luis called.

"I can't." I was alone with the mirrors.

"If I go away, will you come out?"

"No." I closed my eyes. "Where are you?"

"Here behind you. Open your eyes."

"No." I walked with my hands outstretched toward his voice.

"Open your eyes. What are you afraid of?"

"The mirrors. They're all so crazy . . . worse than the one at Aunt Bertha's."

He covered both my hands with his.

I turned around, pushing both his hands aside and opened my eyes to the absolute whiteness of his shirt, then I backed slowly into the room again while looking down at my feet. Dirty. Stockings full of runs. Slowly I raised my eyes to the hem of my skirt, my belt. I circled around and raised my eyes again, this time toward the mirrors. I ran my fingers through my hair.

"I really do look peculiar. Even in a true mirror I would look strange."

Luis shrugged. "So do I." His tall body had been shoved into all the same distortions as mine. I stared at a reflection showing us both too thin on top and shortened at the bottom. Our legs were like Uncle Mowrey's under his newspaper except much shorter and fatter.

"Why does anybody think these are funny?"

Luis shrugged again. "Some people do."

"They're ugly . . . just ugly."

He smiled. "That's part of it . . . part of what we see all the time . . . ugliness, cruelty. . . ."

Death, I thought, but remembering his father didn't say. I turned back to the mirrors glancing at each distorted reflection, so I could see myself as a whole gallery of freaks capriciously designed by a mind I didn't know. Then I looked away from them to different parts of my body, to legs, arms, hands, comparing them to the caricatures I saw against the wall. My own arms and hands were actually thin. I knew my back was straight enough, and I would never weigh 350 pounds.

"Luis, let's get out of here." I picked up my shoes.

He took my hand and led me back through the darkened corridor.

We ordered hamburgers in a diner three or four blocks from the beach. I called Aunt Bertha at the Balinese Room and told the necessary lies . . . that I was sorry, that I'd felt ill and had gone outside for air. Luis didn't try to reach his father. Under the glaring fluorescent lights we drank awful coffee, ate greasy hamburgers with too much mustard on them, wiped our mouths on paper napkins we grabbed from a chrome holder on the table. Still tasting onions and mustard, I vowed our supper was better than anything I could have eaten at the Balinese.

"Want to go back?" Luis offered.

I shook my head. "Not me. You go if you want. I can walk to the house."

"It's too long a walk from here. I'll take you."

It was so dark that night, so black. Streetlights made little pools of yellow we drove through. Luis dropped me off at the Mclean house and went back to his father, back to the Balinese.

Living at the Mcleans' that August continued to be like living through repeated summer storms. Dark gray clouds piled up, sweeping winds blew bursts of rain for a while, then all was quiet again, sunny, calm. Heat crept back over the island. A little breeze blew in from the Gulf.

Emmett lost nearly three hundred dollars playing roulette at the Balinese the night we were there. Bertha didn't appear concerned, nor did Mowrey. Perhaps Bertha had also played and lost. More likely she considered empty pockets the safest solution to Emmett's passion for gambling. The odd part was he'd played at the same table as Luis's father. In four or five spins of the wheel all of his money was swept toward Mr. Platon who, Emmett said, didn't know him from a dog on the street. This contempt was, I thought, only a reflection of Emmett's feelings about someone seeing him lose. For a day or two he seemed contrite.

As for my leaving the club, my aunt and uncle remained mercifully silent. Bertha did ask about my illness. I described a headache and a slightly upset stomach. Too much sun, too many fried shrimp for lunch maybe. "Queasy," was the term I used. I'd been queasy.

Bertha readily accepted the explanation. Like my mother, like all the Chandler women, she believed in the almost magical properties of food. "Something you ate" could be blamed for illness or, on the other hand, could inspire health.

Emmett was harder to deal with.

"You sleeping with that Meskin?"

"Why do you have to call Luis names? He was your friend first."

"That's what he is . . . Meskin."

"His mother was from Galveston. She was born on the island. His father came here from Mexico. Luis was born and brought up here. He went all through school here. So did his brother. He was killed on Guam."

"So he's half a Meskin."

"What difference does it make?"

"You sleeping with him?"

"That's none of your business."

"I thought you came down here to keep me out of trouble."

"Keep your own self, Emmett."

I pulled the sheets off my bed, folded them, and stacked them on top of my pillow. Emmett had followed me back upstairs after breakfast. He'd been kneeling beside his bed going through pockets of the pants he'd stuffed in his suitcase in search of money he might have overlooked. From the bottom of my bed, I caught hold of the spread and pulled it up over the mattress cover. Grabbing up my pillow and sheets, I started out the bedroom door clutching everything in a big messy bunch.

"Where are you going now?"

"That's none of your business either. What I do in the daytime, who I sleep with at night is my concern, not yours, nor anybody else's."

Emmett pulled at one corner of a draggling sheet.

"I don't think you and the Meskin ought to be using Aunt Bertha's bed sheets in the back seat of her car."

He reached for the whole bunch of sheets, but I wheeled away quickly and ran for the stairs. Behind the banister I shouted at him, "You've got an over-sexed imagination, Emmett. Why don't you use it to dream Doris, or Jane, or some other girl is in bed with you every night?"

"How do you know I don't?"

I laughed then, laughed so hard I nearly dropped the pillow and balled up sheets down the length of the stairway.

Peering over the banister with a puzzled look on his face, he hollered, "What's so funny?"

"You are!" Still clutching my bundle, still laughing, I went on downstairs.

Earlier that morning Aunt Bertha had agreed to let me sleep on the living room couch. She'd gotten so accustomed to Mowrey's snores, she confessed, she hadn't even heard Emmett's. Perhaps it would be better for Emmett to take the couch? He usually came in later, didn't he?

I insisted I'd be better than Emmett at keeping the living room presentable.

Bertha smiled and said she supposed so since she knew Emmett didn't know how to make a bed, much less to fold sheets.

I folded and hid the sheets behind my pillow on the couch in Aunt Bertha's cluttered living room, my room now. From the first night I slept better there, even though in that old house with its wooden floors and walls, I could, on still nights, hear both the Mcleans and Emmett rumbling above.

elia, it's your mother!" Aunt Bertha hollered from the top of the stairs.

Mother's voice on the phone sounded strained, "Honey, there was this boy asking for you at the door this morning. Tony . . . Tony Gregory. Isn't he the one from Colorado? I had my hair in pin curls and cold cream all over my face." She half-laughed. "And there he was on the front porch. I thought it was the yard man ringing the bell."

I swallowed and waited. It was around one in the afternoon. Aunt Bertha was probably still awake upstairs, listening maybe.

"He wanted to know where you were. He looked awful. Said he'd been driving all night. I asked him if he wanted to sleep awhile here. No, he just wanted to know how much further it was to Galveston."

I folded myself cross-legged on the floor next to the little table that held the phone. I'd been stretched out on the couch fascinated by an old book called *The Story of the Galveston Flood* written by a newspaper man in 1900, who promised it would be *Complete, Graphic, Authentic.* I'd found it the day I'd been searching for the atlas. When the phone rang I was reading horrifying stories told by survivors, and hated having to put the book down. Now it lay splayed out on the marble-topped coffee table, the cover showing a man in a boat with a rope in his hands looking toward a lot of heads bobbing in the sea. In my chest I had a strange hollow feeling, in my head the same hollowness expanded. I couldn't think. All I could do was stare in the direction of the front door and imagine Tony driving toward Galveston in the black convertible his parents had given him earlier in the summer when he promised to stay in law school. I blinked at the phone's receiver.

"Celia!"

"Yes . . . yes, Mother." What was he doing in Leon? I'd written him, told him I was in Galveston. "Mother, when was he—? What time did he—?"

"About eleven, just about two hours ago. I would have called you then, but I had to run out and stop the yardman. You know how he is. He was supposed to just trim the nandina. He'd nearly cut it to the ground and was moving on to the bridal wreath. I had to tie strings on things to show him where to stop. Then I needed to get lunch ready, so I called you as soon as possible afterward."

It was about seven hours by car to Galveston from Leon. If Tony drove straight down, he'd be there by that evening. If he stopped to rest. . . . He'd driven hundreds of miles already.

"Was anybody with him?"

"I don't know. I don't think so. He really needed some sleep. I don't know which one of us looked worse. He's a good-looking boy, but he's a wreck. I thought I should warn you he was coming your way."

I thanked her, hung up the phone, and went back to the couch like a small dumb animal going back to a familiar spot. Emmett had already gone out prowling around somewhere. Aunt Bertha must have returned to her nap. She'd shouted down to ask if everyone was all right. By that she meant, if no one's injured or dead, don't wake me. Long distance calls, to the Chandlers, generally meant trouble.

Lying on my back, the book open on my chest as though I might weigh the hollowness down with it, I remained numb. For a while I stayed there, breathing normally, but feeling as inert as the carved wooden ladies holding the coffee table on their heads.

When Bertha woke from her nap about two and came down, I went upstairs to reread Tony's last letter, which I'd hidden in my suitcase. He didn't give the slightest hint he'd come. School was still in session. There were no holidays I could think of in August. I remembered Alicia Dorman's letter well enough. Tony was seeing his old girlfriend again, and I'd been sure he was more interested in her availability than in my distance. How could I be responsible for luring him down to Texas? I'd been so unhappy that I hadn't trusted myself to write him after tearing up my angry letter. Had he guessed someone had told me about Judy? I wasn't sure I even wanted him to come. Why was everything so complicated?

I kept going over the hours, the simple mathematics of his arrival in my head. It was one when Mother called after lunch . . . if he'd left Leon when he'd checked by the house around eleven, by six or seven, depending on whether he stopped to eat or sleep and how fast he was driving, he would be in Galveston. There was no way, as much as I tried to guess, to know exactly when he'd be there. Knowing exactly, I was determined, would have helped some, an idea that kept circling around in my head.

Luis called about the movie we were supposed to see that night, a re-run of *Show Boat* that had just come to town. I made excuses. A friend had suddenly decided to drive down. I didn't say whether my friend was male or female, the only dodge I was capable of inventing at the time. I certainly wasn't going to invent a fake cousin.

Aunt Bertha had to be told. On my way to the kitchen I eyed the phone wishing I could talk to Alicia Dorman, but I couldn't call her from the house. In a family where only death and disaster messages were delivered long distance, I couldn't ask permission to phone a friend in Colorado just because I needed to talk, which was all I could admit to Aunt Bertha. I didn't want her to hint to Emmett that Tony was particularly important. He was simply someone I'd known in Colorado who'd decided to come to the coast I said.

"He must have gotten some idea in his head. I didn't ask him to come."

Aunt Bertha gave me a knowing smile. "You're sure you don't want your friend to stay here, Celia? You could move back to that empty bed upstairs, and your friend could have the couch."

The mere idea of going back upstairs to sleep by Emmett's side again made me furious.

"No." I blurted, then caught myself, and added, "No, Aunt Bertha. You've got enough company already. He can stay at a motel . . . the Jack Tar. That's the nearest one, isn't it?"

I edged toward the downstairs bath and jumped into my bathing suit while still talking about how comfortable Tony would be at the motel through the half-closed door. Then I moved out of the side door as fast as I could. I couldn't stand the idea of Tony Gregory staying at the house, not with Emmett hanging around leering and asking rude questions, not with Uncle Mowrey and Aunt Bertha watching our every move. No matter what they might happen to think of him, they would be. . . . Oh, they would be forever there, too close to us in one room or another.

What right had he to turn up without any kind of notice? Why had he gone to Leon when I'd written him two letters from Galveston? Probably it was my fault, or he would say it was. I must have neglected to say how long we were staying. He could have called me in Leon, and Mother would have told him where I was. What kind of surprise did he think he was going to spring on me? Didn't he realize she'd call? Questions swarmed in my head. I couldn't understand why he acted as he did. I never had been able to.

Walking fast toward the Gulf, wearing a beach jacket over my suit, I was carrying only a towel and a few dollars in one pocket. Finally I found a pay phone in a drugstore two blocks from the seawall. It was hidden behind a pile of pink beach balls, the kind people bought for their children when they came down for a weekend, cheap ones they could afford to leave behind or let a sneaky wave steal.

I got some dollars changed and pushed coins in the phone with shaking fingers. In my hurry I dropped two quarters on the floor, so I stood on one while raking the other toward me with my foot. Repeating the number to the operator, I prayed that Alicia would answer. It wasn't likely. There were about fifteen girls living in the same house. I let the phone ring ten times before someone I didn't know told me she was possibly in class. Whole minutes ticked away while I waited for the girl to look around.

"She isn't upstairs," the same voice with a midwestern accent said. "Could I have her call you?"

"Yes. . . . No! Tell her Celia Henderson called. I'll . . . I'll get in touch later."

A clerk, a woman who had a heavy looking pile of dyed black hair spilling around her high pale forehead, the same one that changed dollars for me, asked as I slowly walked out, "You get your call through?"

I nodded. It made no difference whether I had or not. What good would it have done to talk to Alicia? Some. Maybe she could have told me what Tony had been doing lately, if he was still going out with Judy, if he'd said anything about taking off for Texas. What if she didn't know the answers to any of those questions? Talking to her would still have helped; she could have, at least, commiserated. I would have loved talking to Alicia.

I tried to think of Tony as only a boy driving in my direction, a boy who had somehow decided he had to see me. We had agreed he might come down to Texas at Thanksgiving, but that was four months in the future, and the whole trip was totally conditional, based on how one or both of us might feel in November. I'd planned to see him—if he came—on home territory in Leon. Instead he was coming to Galveston which, for me, was uncertain ground at best. Emmett would be hanging around. Aunt Bertha might resume worrying and watching as she did when we first came, and Luis— Where would Luis be in all this?

I walked on down to the Gulf, and without wading around on the long shallow slope, and swam deliberately out to water just above my head. Moving parallel to shore, out of reach of the low tide's waves, I could swim as much and as hard as I wanted and what I wanted was to swim beyond thinking, to be so physically strained my tumbling questions would stop. Unfortunately I found I couldn't swim that hard. The more I decided not to think about Tony showing up, the more I thought about it. By suppertime I couldn't eat.

Emmett noticed; so did Aunt Bertha. Uncle Mowrey either didn't see the plate of food cooling in front of me or tried not to. I was getting ready to leave the table when the front doorbell began ringing.

When I opened it I could see Tony was practically leaning on the bell. I usually got a good deal of pleasure just looking at Tony Gregory. He was tall and fair, and he moved surely, aware of himself but not posturing. His face was generally animated. He smiled easily. Tonight his features were drawn, his forehead flushed with heat, and his chin, lightly stubbled. Fatigue had worn such shadows under his blue eyes that his face looked bruised.

When he saw me he slumped against the doorframe, reached out and put a hand on my shoulder. "Found you."

Unable to say a word, I waited before him, almost paralyzed by conflicting emotions. I'd wanted so much to see him while I'd been so sure I should forget him. I wanted to trust him, but he wasn't trustworthy. Now here he was. I held my right arm out toward him like a child frozen in one of the strange positions we used to assume when we played statues. Impulsively I moved toward him.

Before I could touch him, Aunt Bertha's voice rose behind me. "The poor boy. Bring him in, Celia," she insisted as if she thought I should try to carry him in the house.

I swung the door wide and let Tony step into the hall. Quickly I introduced him to Bertha who was still clucking in the background. "You look exhausted. Come in. Come on in. There's plenty of supper."

He swore he was too worn out to eat. After he made his excuses, I drove him over to the Jack Tar. Its sailing ship sign, placed above the building, blinked on and off making the ship look like it was rocking across neon waves.

"God! Make it quit!" Tony said.

I led him to his room. We didn't say much. He was too weary, and I was still half-numb. Promising to return when he called the next morning, I drove the car back to the Mcleans' house. The black convertible, impractical for traveling, still smelled new even though it had been driven through most of Colorado, the Oklahoma Panhandle and the entire length of droughty dusty Texas.

In the morning Tony was still a little groggy when we met for breakfast, but he was able to tell me before he'd had coffee that he'd quit law school. The course in procedure was more than he could bear. I couldn't tell whether it was the course or his own willingness to quit which decided him. Some of both, I guessed. His parents didn't know yet. He hadn't said anything to them; he just got in his car and drove to Texas to tell me.

We were eating in the same diner Luis had taken me to the night I ran away from the Balinese. Somehow its shabby tidiness was comforting; the row of revolving stools covered with slightly peeling light green plastic, the chrome napkin holders all polished and shining in each booth and, just beyond the last seat at the counter, the pie display—two glass shelves of precise triangles of chocolate meringue, lemon meringue, and cherry with a lattice crust on top—all appeared to promise that someone was in charge, and the day would continue in an ordinary fashion. Tony had already complained that his eggs were too hard, a familiar fault of cooks in Texas as well as those in Colorado. He was lamenting fry cooks in general when a big broad-chested man who might have been a truck driver or a wharf worker came in. Obviously a regular, he said "Morning," to the waitress who immediately placed a cup of coffee in front of him. Surrounded by calm, I grew calmer.

After he'd finished his coffee, Tony reached across the table and took my hand. "I guess I should have told you, should have called and told you I was coming."

"Why didn't you?"

"I couldn't take the time—"

"But you had to stop now and then."

"Celia, I can't explain it. You…you were out there, out in front of me. That's all I could think about."

I was flattered, then angry at him all over again. Sitting in the same place where I'd sat letting Luis comfort me, I could feel my contrary impulses rising. I wanted Tony to be there, and I wanted him gone.

"Let's go back to the room." He pulled a *Do Not Disturb* sign out of his back pocket and grinned.

I shook my head. I was mad at Tony, mad at myself. Earlier I wished for him, yearned for him. If he'd been there a week before, if he'd gone with us to the Balinese Club, I would have stayed on the dance floor next to him. Now, across the table from him, I chewed hard on a piece of toast and tried to wash it down with tepid coffee. So many miles away from me, he'd been a memory; here he was a lover, one I realized I'd begun to put aside. I'd almost escaped when he turned up to make demands. Anger made me wary. I wouldn't go back to his room with him. Instead, keeping well away from Luis's house on West Beach, I showed Tony the Galveston Luis had shown me.

We walked almost to the end of the pier Luis and I had walked, drove to the wharves, took the ferry to Bolivar, ate lunch at Gaido's. Tony was interested only in the food and drink. He was pleased to be able to stroll into a bar at noon and order Scotch before lunch. Other than that, the pier was boring, the sea, a strange sandy brown, the wharves were nothing more than stink and decay. The ferry, though a relief from the heat, was repetitious. Tony chaffed against everything except the one bar I took him to and Gaido's which he found civilized. Despite the picnics we'd had in Colorado and the two brief hikes we'd done in Estes Park, Tony didn't really like the outdoors. He vastly preferred being in any air-conditioned room, preferably a bar or bedroom, and he would not really talk to me about his future. If I brought up cooking schools, he said the Cordon Bleu was in Paris, which was too far away from me. As for those in this country, he couldn't think of one in Texas. Law school couldn't be discussed. Texas was too hot and dry; otherwise he rather liked the state. He had no intention of calling home anytime soon. Perhaps I should call. It was my fault he was there, he teased. Without ever mentioning the motel room again, he cajoled. And I decided, yes, I still yearned for Tony. I understood that he was more worn out and more worried than he cared to show. Even if he didn't see the city as I did, I still liked watching him move, seeing his eyes crinkle when he laughed, feeling his arm around me.

I told him, of course, I still loved him. At the same time I told myself I couldn't trust him. He was way too unhappy, too moody. He'd quit school, gotten in a car and driven two days to see me without bothering to call first. He'd pulled off to the side of the road, slept four or five hours in his car, washed his face in filling station men's rooms, eaten in cafes he could neither remember nor wanted to remember. All this I was supposed to understand, even to admire the hardships he'd gone through to reach me but why, I asked again, couldn't he have used just one telephone in all three states he passed through?

"What if I weren't in Texas? I could have gone back to Tennessee to visit?" We were walking back to the car from Gaido's. The afternoon sun soaked the asphalt in the parking lot, bounced off the cars around us.

He smiled. "You were though. You wrote me from Galveston. I went to Leon first because you didn't say how long you were staying."

"That is so crazy! What if you'd gotten here, and I was involved with someone else?"

"I would have turned around and gone back," he said, laughed and added he didn't think I was.

I didn't tell him about Luis. What was there to tell? We'd spent some time together. Tony had been spending time with someone else. Judy? She was just someone he knew, had known for years, an old flame, an old friend, someone to have a beer with now and then. I was the one he had to see. Romantic as it appeared, I couldn't believe him. What was he trying to prove to me, to himself? I wouldn't go back to the Jack Tar with him. I could see him only if he would give up trying to get me to bed.

"We've been so near to it, we might as well have slept together. . . ."

"I can't stand worrying about pregnancy for weeks."

"I can use something."

"Girls get pregnant, even with . . . with rubbers."

"You won't."

"You don't know. You can't make that kind of promise."

He was furious. So was I. We were caught in a trap we'd made for ourselves. I thought perhaps he'd leave. Instead he took me to the Mcleans' late that afternoon. I knew I couldn't sleep, and I didn't want to have to talk to Aunt Bertha so I got in the tub and stayed as long as possible trying to soak away weariness.

In an hour he was back. We sat in his car next to the big palm. I saw he was as miserable as I was, and I still couldn't bear the idea of him driving off alone. He wouldn't go with me to the beach or to a bar. I agreed to go to the motel with him. We would not make love, he promised.

Trying not to grin, he hung the *Do Not Disturb* sign on the doorknob. The room was dark. The long twilight had begun; little glimmers of daylight mixed with neon from the ship sign crept around the edges of the curtains. The bed was neatly made. He'd been there taking a shower, he said.

I laughed thinking how we'd both been under water while we were apart. There was only one chair in the room. I sat down on the edge of it while he mixed a Scotch and soda.

He sat on the bed drinking quickly, watching me, saying little, then quite deliberately, put the glass down on the nightstand.

"Come here."

I shook my head.

He walked over to me, knelt and began untying the shirt-tail knot I'd made in front. I'd changed into a fresh shirt and shorts, the same sort of clothes I'd worn every day on the island.

No one had totally undressed me since I was a child. We had almost made love, our clothes half on, half off, somewhere in Estes Park one rainy afternoon. I remembered he had the same expertise before. I remembered also that we hadn't even kissed each other but once since he arrived.

I brushed his hands away when he started unbuttoning my shirt.

"I'm not going to be the only one naked," I said.

"I want to look at you . . . just to look."

"Not with all your clothes on."

"Why not?" He pulled me up to him by both hands.

"It's unfair somehow."

"There's nothing fair about this."

"I know." I twisted away from him. "I can't get near a bed with you. Come on."

He left me standing at the foot of the bed, sat down on it, groaned, stood up, walked over to me and said, "I'm going to hate myself for this the rest of my life. This is the most perverse thing I've ever—"

Perhaps it was. I didn't know. I wasn't even sure what he meant.

We kissed until our mouths were dry, our lips bruised. His hands moved over my back, down my arms lightly, slowly.

Abruptly, using both hands on his chest, I pushed myself away.

He reached toward me, but I was close enough to the door to turn and run out of the room. Hardly seeing, without thinking, I fled across the street to the seawall. I could hear Tony calling my name as I rushed down the cement steps to the beach to face the dark water. Tears ran down my cheeks. I didn't want him to see me crying, to guess how much I wanted to turn back and run toward him.

Without speaking, he followed me. We must have walked along the beach silently for a quarter of a mile until I recognized a stairway on the seawall, took it, took the street directly across the boulevard and kept walking toward the Mclean house.

Tony turned away when he saw the direction I'd chosen, and started toward the motel. Above his head I watched the ship sailing ,the three rippled lines of pink, blue and white neon sea blinking in the night sky.

In the final block before reaching the house, I thought, "At least I still have my clothes on." I was glad I did even if I would have been glad to have had them off earlier. Then I remembered all the names boys called girls who wouldn't give in. "Pricktease" came to mind most often. He was right. There was nothing fair about it.

The next day he came by so early he had to talk to Aunt Bertha while I left the breakfast table to run upstairs and dress. I'd thought I would never see him again, that he'd leave without a word. Had he realized, perhaps, that I felt as miserable as he did?

From the bathroom window I could see Emmett outside inspecting the convertible's motor. Heavier, a little taller, obviously darker, his shaggy hair growing straight over the back of his neck, he gestured toward the engine, touching it here and there, almost patting it. I'd watched Kenyon act the same way when he looked at a friend's new car.

Tony, his light hair catching the sun, reached beyond him to close the hood with a pleased look on his face.

Emmett laughed.

I had tried to keep them apart. When Tony arrived I got him away from the house before I even had to introduce him to Emmett. Now they turned to lounge against the convertible's side next to the curb as if they were two old friends. They both liked fast cars. Emmett had already been warned against hot-rodding around Galveston in Bertha's well-known Chrysler. By the time I joined them Emmett was offering to take Tony to some of the places he knew.

"What do you like, five card stud, draw—?"

"I don't gamble." Tony put his arm around me and drew me close.

I almost jumped. His moods changed so quickly I couldn't gauge them. Was he here because he'd forgiven me, or because he just couldn't decide what he wanted to do next?

"There's a game going on around Galveston nearly anytime if you change your mind," Emmett offered again.

Tony shook his head. "I don't like losing money on dogs, horses, or cards. The odds are always rigged against you. The house always gets paid."

Emmett grinned. "I don't figure to win all the time. Ask Celia."

Tony pulled me tighter against his side.

"He loses pretty often," I said.

"Yeah. Well . . . by the time we go home, I could even be ahead." Emmett laughed as if he was laughing at himself.

"Or behind," Tony said quietly but his contempt could be heard.

I wasn't sure Emmett had noticed.

He shrugged and stepped back a little, so I could see his face more clearly. His expression was amiable, too amiable, too calm. His eyes met mine. He gave me a quick sideways glance indicating I was to move.

I didn't believe he'd hit him, but I wasn't altogether certain. Tony was tall but slight, and he was a guest, someone who'd just come to get me at our aunt's house. Clearly Emmett wanted me to stand aside. Standing as close as I could to Tony, I waited. It was so quiet I could hear a little breeze shuffling through the palm leaves.

Tony started opening the door on my side. "Come on," he said.

Emmett, his back to us, stalked toward the west porch door.

"Your cousin—" he complained as we drove off. His mood had veered once more. Now he was angry and wanted to be soothed.

I saw the question in his eyes and answered before he asked. "We barely manage to get along."

"I bet. Women are crazy about cowboys."

"Oh, God, Tony!" Since he'd gone to school in Colorado, a state so western I thought he'd understand. Surely I didn't have to tell him there was a cowboy of some sort on every street corner in Leon.

He went on talking about Emmett, my sexy cousin, living in the same house and going everywhere with me. By the time we got to the seawall, he'd convinced himself he was jealous of Emmett. He refused to understand me.

Tony turned right on the boulevard and followed the seawall discovering, as he drove, the road down the west side of the island. Luis lived in one of the few beach houses out there. The rest of that end of the island was taken up by the country club, a skeet club, a few family camps—wooden houses on stilts with screened-in sleeping porches—and farms. The first one we drove by, a dairy farm reeking of manure, was the most noticeable. Another held Laffite's Grove, a clump of trees on slightly higher ground, one of the sites where Laffite's treasure was supposedly buried. Luis had told Emmett about it the first day they met in the beer joint on the beach. Emmett announced he would dig there immediately, then got too drunk to do anything. When he'd sobered up the next day Uncle Mowrey, finding him in the garage looking for a shovel, told him Laffite's Grove had been dug up often enough already. And it was on private land.

I wondered if Tony and I might pass Luis driving in from his house to town. Not likely. And even if we did Tony would never guess I was far more interested in Luis than Emmett. We drove by the little road leading off to Luis' place so fast no one could have possibly recognized me in sunglasses, a scarf knotted under by chin, wrapped around my neck, and tied behind my head again. I had stuck it in the glove box earlier that summer. When I first saw that piece of white silk again I remembered wearing it nearly every time we went out while I was in Colorado and was foolishly pleased simply because Tony still carried my scarf around.

"Watch this," he commanded. Flooring the gas pedal, he pointed to the speedometer. When it hit 110, the land merged into a blur and I began shouting at him to slow down. I knew that road, and we were coming to the end of it. Not so far in front of us was nothing but sand and a sheet of bay water.

"It'll do 120," he shouted as if I couldn't read a speedometer.

I slid down further into the seat and shouted back. "Who cares?"

"I do."

"I don't. Stop it, Tony." I screamed against the wind.

He slowed the car. "I'm going to give the damn car back to my parents. I just wanted to show you what it could do."

I unwound the white scarf and stuck it back in the glove compartment without saying anything. I hated the avid look on his face.

"Chicken."

"That's me."

"Mad?"

"Listen! I'm scared of lots of things, of seas too high, water too rough, jellyfish, people who drive too fast! I have a right to be scared!" I shouted at him, at anyone nearby.

"Okay, okay, Celia. What else is there to do here beside playing poker with your cousin?"

I ignored his sneer and talked him into wading in the surf with me. He had already adamantly refused to swim in the Gulf. "It's dirty," he kept saying.

I looked at him standing on the shore, his pants legs rolled up, a city boy unhappy outdoors.

"It's only sand. The slope is so gentle the waves stir it up as they come in and deposit it again when the tide is higher. Look, the last little wave is clear."

"It's looks dirty." There was a petulant tone to his voice. His face was flushed with heat and sun. Just briefly in the harsh light, I saw him as a truculent little boy digging his heels in the sand and refusing to get wet mainly because some adult, his mother or his father most likely, wanted him to. It seemed he couldn't finish growing up, and as much as I hoped he might someday, I couldn't believe it would happen anytime soon.

He trudged over the sand to his car to reach in the back seat for a bottle of Scotch he'd left there in a sack. He held it out toward me.

I shook my head. I didn't want a drink. It was eleven in the morning on a clear, bright day. I'd had enough to drink the day before. Tony was never far from a bottle of something.

I couldn't truly understand him, nor could I help him. He wasn't helping me. When I went off to college— really some years before that—I'd sworn not to marry before finishing. I'd seen enough girls staying home with babies. No one I knew went on to college after a shotgun wedding. Abortions were illegal; they only took place in stories. And in every one of them I'd read, the girls bled to death or died of a terrible infection. Most of all, I didn't want to have to marry anyone. Continually pulled between wanting Tony and worry over getting caught, my stomach remained in a coil. I still couldn't eat much; I could hardly sleep at all. Both nights he'd been there I had tried the couch and the floor.

Later that afternoon he drove me back to the house. The two of us sat in his car under the palm tree looking at each other.

"You never loved me," he said, his voice bitter, his face taut.

All I could say was, "I did."

Chapter Nine

In the mornings Emmett slept later and later. I became the restless one. I'd avoided seeing Luis when Tony was in town and now found myself usually on my own. Perhaps Luis had discovered someone else to spend time with; perhaps he'd begun to paint all day. For the first time in years, I had whole days to myself. I began to leave the house early for exploratory walks in the neighborhood before the sun got too hot. Going east I paused to stare through the dark windows of small Italian grocery stores where dim lights showed rows of vegetables—zucchini, tomatoes, lettuce—with stalks of yellowing bananas swaying over them. Young mothers were out pushing their babies in strollers. An old man carrying a newspaper in a neat roll under one arm must have been hurrying home to read it. For a block or so I was followed by various stray dogs who invariably deserted me for familiar whistles. In the afternoons I sometimes found refuge in the Rosenberg, Galveston's library. It had a faint sweet smell of old wood mixed with floor wax and the same sort of furniture polish used by all the libraries I'd known in all the places I'd ever lived.

I checked out *Kon-Tiki* and *From Here to Eternity* and read them together alternating between the voyage and the tragedy mixing fact with fiction, delight with doom. In the library I found old pictures of people walking through the city on boards ten feet high in the air. "The Raising of Galveston," a large caption read. Too low, always in danger of flooding, the whole city had been raised. Houses, even churches, divided into sections behind dikes, were jacked up, so everyone moved on high boardwalks to enter their homes. In the old sepia-toned pictures the walkways looked so narrow that the little stick figures of people suspended on them seemed in danger of falling every moment. I could see the wavering lines of sewers, water, and gas raised also.

"But what made the ground rise?" I had to ask Uncle Mowrey.

"It was all part of a plan. They dredged wet sand from the harbor's channel, moved it through canals cut through the island, then pumped it out on land. Water from the sand drained away. The island rose."

To me it was almost magical. How did they, I wondered, ever get everyone to agree to suspend their houses, their whole lives like that?

"They didn't have to," said Mowrey. The 1900 storm did it . . . built the seawall, raised the city too." Abruptly he fell into silence again. He liked passing on bits of information, but I found I had to ask precise questions.

It must have been something more, I thought, something more than the storm . . . people's stubbornness, pride . . . a will to resist that made them search for a way. Of course their homes were there, and so were their livelihoods. I'd seen hundreds of people move during the war. That was different; those were temporary shifts, or so most of them believed, so I had believed when the war began. Those who'd stayed in Galveston after the storm— Weren't many of them immigrants, people who had already chosen to make one great move? Had they simply decided, once they were settled, to stay put? Whatever their reasons, they had been determined to live on higher ground.

I'd walk carrying my library books to and from the Mclean's looking for signs of the raising but never found any. The landscape had been completely replaced. All the trees had died in the sand they pumped in. New trees and gardens grew on soil hauled from the mainland. So here was Galveston, once an island with only three trees on it, now covered with acres of greenery.

Always I was drawn back to the seawall across Broadway past the Church of the Sacred Heart, past the Bishop's Palace and Lucas Terraces with its shell-shaped window boxes, past the little cottages raised high on piers to the sometimes brown-gray, sometimes gray-green Gulf. The part of the beach that lay parallel to the Mcleans' was lined with souvenir shops and hung with swags of net holding dried starfish. Giant conch shells collected, I supposed, from remote islands lay stacked in curling heaps around steps and doors. These were particularly beautiful. Perhaps I thought so because they were familiar. A conch shell stood gathering dust on top of a bookcase on the landing of the stairs at Grandmother Henderson's house. My father showed me how to hold it to my ear and listen for the sea's roar. On clear days the heaps of conches with their pink and orange spirals shimmered. I watched children holding them to their ears, recognized the smiles coming to their faces while their parents waited silently, delighting in passing on an old secret.

My own parents had given that secret to me. What else had I been taught? Don't take candy from strangers, don't get into cars with strangers, don't be afraid of policemen— So many don'ts. So many instructions, all of them parts of an old set of cautions handed down every generation the same way *Mother Goose* rhymes were repeated and the gift of the sea sounding conch was given.

Mother taught me the nursery rhymes, gave me a *A Child's Garden of Verses,* read the Greek myths to me as well as the fairy tales; she'd shown me how to tie Kenyon's shoes and zip up his jacket, how to make a bed and set a table. She'd shown me how to ride a bicycle too since my father was in the army by the time I got one. What about all the things I couldn't remember being taught like how to hold a knife and fork or to dress myself? So much forgotten....

Kenyon had just as many lessons too. What was keeping him so unhappy for so long? Was it my father's disciplined rule, his demand for obedience and grades, not even good grades anymore just passing grades, that drove Kenyon to sullen withdrawal and near failure? How odd that my father could accommodate any amount of eccentricity in his friends but couldn't allow the least deviation in his son. Yet he spent time with him, taught Kenyon to hunt, took him on fishing trips to the mountains, found him summer jobs, worried about him all the time.

Kenyon was smart enough and strangely patient with animals. He'd found a crow with a lame leg, bound it up, trained it to light on his arm, but once it was well, he wouldn't return the bird to the cage he'd built. The raccoon he wanted to tame used the toilet bowls to wash his paws in. Mother couldn't stand that. He taught our father's bird-dog how to shake hands and to fetch the evening newspaper. The bird flew off, the raccoon went back to the river bank, the bird-dog, chasing the paper which landed in the street, was run over. Kenyon joined the track team, the only team he was ever on. He was good at running. He'd outrun the cops who came after him for flinging horse apples from the roof at people leaving the football stadium in Leon.

There was no knowing the sources of his wildness. Emmett could be just as wild . . . just as self-destructive, and in contrast to my father, Uncle Estes, like a lot of farmers and ranchers during the war, never left home. Boys would be boys, he must have said that or something like it as he rode off to check the cattle.

Neither he nor my father could talk about their feelings. My father tended to anesthetize his with alcohol. Estes took the distant path. Amiable, detached, he was there, and he wasn't there. In that family Earlene was the one with feelings on the surface. Among the Chandlers, women cried and carried on all they pleased. They sorrowed with you and for you, and they comforted. Aunt Bertha, I guessed, was waiting, knowing she'd be needed.

Luis, except for his worry about his father, seemed more carefree. Certainly he was calmer than Emmett or my brother.

When I told him so, he laughed.

"No, I've just got a different set of problems."

I'd begun to sense he was right, but—other than his father's prolonged mourning—I couldn't understand what they were, nor could I ask outright. It was too bold a question, too prying. I dawdled along the beach holding my sandals in my hand sighing over things that couldn't be said. There were mysteries everyone carried with them, and whatever Luis's were, they remained his.

Standing on top of the seawall by the souvenir shop, I stared at the swimmers and sunbathers spread out on the gray-brown sand below. No cars were allowed on this part of the beach. Umbrellas and floats had to be rented. Cold drinks could be bought from vendors. People arrived with nothing on but bathing suits, sandals, and shirts. Most carried towels, lotions, books, sunglasses. Down on West Beach where cars were allowed some families planted poles, erected tents, and, when everything had been unlocked and put in place, recreated houses without walls where their dogs ran gleefully in and out. Whether they went to little trouble or a lot everybody got tanned or sunburned during the day and went home with a little sand in their shoes. They were all unknown, unnamed to me, and in that private yet public place, to each other, and all of them were playing peaceably at the water's edge, or so it appeared from the top of the seawall.

A little boy dressed in blue shorts and a red striped shirt ran in front of me pushing a stroller.

"Wait, Henry!" called a young woman in a white uniform behind him.

He waited till she caught up with him then climbed in the stroller backward so he was facing her.

I laughed. I could stand on top of walls, lean over balconies, look out of towers, but I couldn't remain at a distance long. There was always something, or someone who caught my eye; a woman passing by in a yellow hat so large it flapped around her face, a boy whistling a tune I recognized. Even the most naked of bathers had some distinguishing mark; an old lady going in the water wearing her pearls just as Bertha wore hers when she went swimming because, she maintained, it was good for them to return to their natural element, a man whose eyebrows met in the middle of his forehead, a small girl about nine proudly wearing a new two-piece swim suit although she had no reason to wear anything on top. I saw them all and wondered about them as I would probably wonder about strangers the rest of my life.

Luis found me there. Bertha had told him she thought I was at the beach, so he'd come to search for me.

"What are you doing here this late in the day? Don't you know you're too young and tender to stay out in the sun?" He smiled as he repeated the phrase used by the old guard we'd seen at the wharves.

It was as if we'd spent all the days before together. I noticed he usually reacted this way. Absences were barely acknowledged, excuses seldom made. Life flowed on; he and his friends would eventually catch up. Then everything would go on as it had before. Luis might sometimes say he missed me, but the fact that I was present was more important.

Early one morning Leslie came by with an extra bike she'd borrowed on a carrier with hers. We went riding west toward San Luis Pass, past the farms, past a couple of old camps on our right, a few beach houses on our left. She stopped at the road to Luis's.

"You want to go down and see him?"

"No. He paints a lot at night, sleeps late most mornings. It's only nine now."

"You like him, don't you?"

"Yes."

"Everybody seems to."

I sensed she was being careful not to say too much. She was looking directly at me, her eyes on my face, so I admitted I didn't know about him, not yet.

"The thing is— Nobody really knows him since he's only here in the summers, and he spends so much time by himself or with his father—"

"I met him the other night at the Balinese. He can't seem to give up his grief, can he?"

"I guess. Everybody just watches him gamble. That's what he can't give up. It's strange. People here— Here everybody bets on horses maybe, plays the slots a little. There's always a poker game going on. Nobody plays like he does.

Even the Maceos have tried to discourage him."

"You're kidding."

"No. It's the truth. My father told my brother they talked to him."

Remembering the money Emmett had lost to him at the roulette table, I wondered if Mr. Platon stuck to only one kind of game. Leslie said he played craps too. She didn't play anything. She'd lost her allowance in the slots when she was eleven. Since then she'd stayed away.

"I don't have money to spend like that. And that's what you're doing really. In the end they win, or they wouldn't stay in business."

"What about luck?" I was thinking of Emmett's belief that his chances were always changing that he might be the lucky one.

Leslie laughed. "The lucky ones quit while they're ahead. I didn't ever get there."

She'd been lucky in a way, I thought, to know she had to quit before she was seized by the fever Emmett had caught, but I didn't mention him. Emmett had been drunk on chance. He was lucky he ran out of money. I'd never played anything except a few slot machines, and I'd found I didn't like being drunk. That was my luck.

We finished eating our sandwiches while sitting on the beach and threw crusts to gulls that plunged after them like zany acrobats.

"It would be harder to ride all day somewhere else. It's so flat here."

"In Europe everybody rides bicycles," Leslie said. "You can take them on trains when you get tired of riding."

The idea of biking around Europe appealed to me though I wasn't certain I could do it. Leslie assured me I could if I rode some every day before going. "European bikes have gears. That makes it easier."

A lot of people in my family had already been. One aunt who had only gone to England and Ireland was dying to go to the continent; my father, though he had a dim view of foreign travel, had wandered through France and Spain; Aunt Bertha, mainly interested in finding the best stores to buy linens and china from, had gone to Cuba with Mother, and to England, and to France. The Chandlers' greatest traveler, she could have easily shopped at home but preferred to buy abroad. There was more to choose from there. So far Uncle Mowrey hadn't gone with her; he hated shopping.

I wasn't interested in shopping either. I started wondering about places I'd only seen pictures of, about different languages, about going to the great museums to look at real paintings instead of reproductions, about history written in stone buildings. To me Europe had begun to mean authentication, and the more I talked to Leslie, the more I wanted to know. We both had all sorts of questions about what was beyond the sea's flat horizon.

Emmett, Aunt Bertha discovered, wasn't seeing anybody but Jane. One evening she wouldn't let him have the car. From that time on, Jane arrived in her own car, which Emmett always drove.

"Out of the frying pan . . ." Aunt Bertha murmured.

"I don't know about that. Doris Lacey is altogether different. She might marry him. I don't know that Jane would."

Bertha, busy defrosting the refrigerator, jabbed at the ice with a butcher knife. She hadn't bothered to take the food off the shelves though she'd removed the ice trays. They were melting in puddles on the kitchen table. I watched her narrowly miss slicing through the eggs in their cardboard box when she suddenly turned to talk to me.

"He's out with her nearly every night."

I nodded. Emmett tended to concentrate on one girl at time.

Aunt Bertha poked away at the ice. "His mother isn't going to be happy about this."

"We'll be gone in a week. Luis and I run into them together some nights. I don't think— Aunt Bertha, doesn't your maid come tomorrow?"

"You're right." She scraped a small pile of ice shavings into her hands and kicked the refrigerator door shut.

It wasn't that Emmett refused friendship with others. There was just no one as easily available to him at that time but Jane. Roby and he had too little in common. As for Marion, he was too much of a baby, and he'd left for Canada with his family anyway. Sometimes when I was with Roby and Leslie or with Luis I would see Emmett at a table with Jane, his hat on the table, his legs stretched out before him relaxing like a cowhand who'd just ridden into town.

Jane leaned forward listening to him, nodding now and then, her honey colored hair gleaming in whatever light was shining. She could make Emmett laugh. Something about her, her slow but insistent disbelief in whatever he was trying to talk her into, her quick affectation of ignorance delighted him.

She would draw me into a conversation almost as soon as she caught sight of me. Luis too. We ran into Jane and Emmett at The Pirate's Den often.

"Where have youall been?" She asked as if she was dying to know. "Where have youall been all night?"

"Nowhere . . . the movies." I said.

"Nobody goes to the movies."

"We have been." Luis grinned. He liked teasing Jane.

"Lu-is! I can't believe you took this girl to a movie! Emmett, what do you think?"

"She goes to them in Leon." He pulled out a chair for me, something I couldn't remember him doing before.

I looked up at him thinking it was the first time I'd seen him really awake in days.

Luis sat across the table from him next to Jane.

"But you don't spend your time going to movies in Galveston, do you, Celia?"

"We were just at the Martini," Luis said.

"I thought you'd be showing her the sights, Luis. Emmett always says, 'Show me the sights, honey.' But he only likes the inside of bars. I can't remember what the inside of anything else looks like except maybe a swimming pool."

Emmett touched her shoulder before interrupting, another small gesture new to him. "What are youall drinking?"

His mother would have been proud of his manners. He seemed to have forgotten he'd ever quarreled with me about Luis or called him a spic. He watched Jane, kept his voice low, and appeared to be listening to the singer if there was one. There would be a piano player, or in some bars, a three man combo—sax, bass, and drums. Mostly though lone piano players sat in dark corners playing to themselves.

To a majority of the customers music was strictly background noise for drinking or gambling. Unless there was a fistfight or a knifing, nobody was going to interrupt that, and in the bars we went to, there were no knifings or fights. They had elaborate names, but plain interiors. There was nothing piratical about The Pirates' Den, nothing harem-like about Omar's. The Balinese Club was an opulent island; the places we went to were places anybody could go to for a drink. Nobody carried whisky in paper sacks in Galveston. No waitress ever asked me my age. I passed for twenty-one easily, however I still had an explorer's taste for exotic cocktails and seldom ordered the same thing twice. Luis, though he ordered for me, never drank anything but bourbon and soda. At The Pearl Diver one night I drank a Brandy Alexander served in a large snifter. At 88 Keys I asked for something called a French 75 which arrived in a tall fluted glass carried by a curious waitress who hung around to watch my reaction. I offered her a taste, but she said she couldn't drink while working. Another night at The Carousel I sipped a Moscow Mule from a copper mug. I tried all these after reading the recipes in Aunt Bertha's *Old Mr. Boston Drinkbook*, which I found poked between cookbooks in her kitchen. I must have stumbled across a classic, for the bartenders in Galveston evidently used the same book.

Luis thought I liked the names of drinks and shapes of containers better than the drinks themselves. Emmett and Jane kept to bourbon and water, however Jane—whenever we joined them—would demand, "Oh, please order something with a parasol in it, Celia."

That night at The Pirate's Den I ordered a Pink Lady.

"There's no parasol in one of those," Jane wailed. "I know. My mother drinks them. Oh, here's Roby. He'll know what comes with one. He knows things like that."

Roby followed Leslie to our table. I glanced over at Emmett who moved his hat off the table and got up to get a chair for Leslie. His glass was still almost half full and it was eleven already. Was he learning to pace himself? I'd discovered I could have one, maybe two drinks if I drank slowly. The night I drank three I was disgustingly sick in an equally disgustingly smelly filling station ladies' room. Emmett had terrible hang-overs. So did I until I decided to drink less.

Roby couldn't think of a drink that came with a parasol except a Singapore Sling, and I wouldn't ask for one of those. There were too many different kinds of liquor in it.

I wondered sometimes if Luis, older than the rest of us, might be bored sitting in bars while I tried different drinks, however he seemed pleased to indulge me when he wasn't working, or—more frequently lately—when he decided he wouldn't go with his father to the Balinese Club.

There was a woman, Mrs. Finley, a widow Luis's mother's age, who went out with Mr. Platon some evenings. She was a secretary, accustomed to other people's whims, Luis said. Obliging. Yes, Mrs. Finley knew how to cater to people. He spoke of her in a dry manner as if merely reporting what his father had been doing lately. When I asked if he liked her, he refused to say. She was an old friend of his parents, he commented. He didn't talk about people much. Those his age, friends he'd had in high school had long since dispersed; only a few of them came back to the island to live.

Roby was the one who kept us occupied, the one who decided we should all ride the roller coaster at the carnival across from the seawall or the bumper cars in the amusement park at Stewart's Beach down on the east end of the island. None of them went to the beach otherwise. I could talk Leslie into going swimming with me occasionally, but Jane wouldn't, nor would have Marion, and Roby wouldn't consider going in the Gulf unless he was fishing or crabbing. The beach had always been there. They had grown up on it. Two or three times we all drove out to the country club to swim. But that had always been there too.

Roby decided we needed to go somewhere else one night when we were all in The Pirates' Den. Everyone went with him for a walk on the seawall. Emmett and Jane lagged behind. They caught up at the steps in front of the souvenir shop where the conch shells were displayed in the daytime.

Cal was there, his fingers lightly tapping his drum, its yellow, red, black, and white zigzags gleaming in the moonlight.

"Tom-Tom!" Roby shouted. There were times his exuberance overflowed, and he'd holler people's names. No one ever minded. Roby knew people liked to hear their names; it made little difference if they were murmured or shouted.

"His name is Cal." I whispered to Luis. "Why does Roby call him Tom-Tom?"

Luis shrugged. "He makes up things, I guess."

Cal grinned at us. He'd quit playing and pushed the drum aside. The moon was coming up late.

"You going to sing for us?" Roby asked him.

"Why not you?"

Roby shook his head, then turning as if he'd just seen him, said, "Emmett will sing!"

Emmett staggered up the steps to the souvenir shop, his boots making a loud clonking sound on the wooden boards, and sat down hard. I hadn't thought he was that drunk.

Cal rolled the drum over toward him.

Holding onto it with one hand, Emmett wobbled to his feet, looked up as though he needed to be sure where the light was coming from, and sang:

Buffalo gals, won't you come out tonight
Come out tonight, come out tonight?
Buffalo gals, won't you come out tonight
And dance by the light of the moon?

He let go of the barrel and lifted his chin to sing in a clear light tenor that carried well. The moon shone in his face, and the waves lapped the sand below the seawall behind him, but he might as well have been in the middle of a corral at the ranch for all he seemed to care.

Cal rolled the barrel closer to himself, and began beating it in time to the tune Emmett had chosen.

"I didn't know he could sing," Jane said.

"I don't think he can, not unless he's drunk," I warned her.

With the sea breeze ruffling his long hair, Emmett sang the same verse again.

We all applauded.

"It's the only verse he knows," I said to Jane. "You'd better turn him off."

Buffalo gals— Emmett began again.

Jane reached for his hand. "Come on."

"I'm singing for you."

"Yes," said Jane, "you're singing for everybody." She led him down the steps.

Roby handed Cal some money. Other people had gathered around us, some of them just as drunk as Emmett was. A man behind me was arguing about the words to *The Streets of Laredo* and getting them wrong. The woman he was arguing with was getting them wrong too, and the man on the other side of her kept agreeing with both of them.

"This going to be a good night." Cal threw back his head and laughed.

Leslie pulled Roby by the hand and whispered something to him. We all started to walk to a cafe for coffee.

"I hate coffee," Emmett complained loudly.

"Oh, hush!" Jane began singing in a wavering soprano, *Shine on. Shine on harvest moon.*

Leslie joined in, and so did I. We walked in a straggling line to the cafe singing all the moon songs we knew. People driving by honked and waved. It was one of the most peaceful nights we spent on the island.

Chapter Ten

There were signs of a storm beginning the afternoon I drove out to see Luis on a whim. I hadn't seen him in two days. Someone else's red sports car, an Austin Healey, was parked next to his black MG in the garage provided by the tall pilings under the house. I ran up the side steps to the deck and found his front door closed which was odd. It had been open every time I'd been there. He disliked carrying things in his pockets so generally left the house unlocked. There was little in it he minded losing. Big canvases were hard to haul away; if anyone wanted a picture badly enough to steal it, they were welcome. I knocked and tried to peer in the broad front window. His bamboo blind had been pulled down. Perhaps he was still asleep. No, not by three in the afternoon. I couldn't hear anyone moving around inside. Was he at the beach? He didn't usually swim at that time. Early in the morning or late in the afternoon after four—those were his choices. But maybe . . . maybe he went for a walk before the storm. He liked the Gulf's dramatic weather. I went to the deck's railing to stare up and down the beach. Of course I couldn't really see far. From there people were just figures, small dark moving shapes, but surely I could discern his. I would recognize him anywhere. Running back to the door, I knocked again. Again there was no answer. This time I thought I heard something, some small movement. I became utterly convinced Luis was in his house . . . Luis and someone else.

I turned and ran down the wooden stairway, the wind pushing at my back, rippling my shirt.

"Fool!" I said aloud. "Fool!" I had come uninvited, and was obviously not welcome. What had I expected? I felt small and ridiculous as if I had been caught spying on someone.

By the time I returned to the Mclean house it was raining hard. Gusts of wind shoved the wiper blades erratically across the windshield, and when I turned the key off all I could see was water-splotched glass. For a few minutes I waited hoping the rain would slacken then decided I'd rather be wet than sit in the closed steamy car any longer. Running to the house I tripped over some scattered bits of loose oyster shell and almost fell. The side door was nearest, but it was locked. Unfortunately the portico offered no real shelter. I pushed the bell. Most of the mechanical devices at the Mcleans' barely worked at all. The iron had a short in it that gave me slight shocks every time I tried to use it. Toilets sighed and had to have handles jiggled. Though the washing machine ran, something had happened to the clothes dryer. Aunt Bertha used a line in the tiny backyard. Every fan except the ceiling fans in the bedrooms growled when turned on, and if anyone made the terrible mistake of switching on the garbage disposal, we all had either to leave the house or endure a ferocious grinding noise until the plumber came. The doorbell, however, worked well. Wet and angry, I leaned against it.

Emmett pulled the door open fast. In one hand he held a telephone receiver. "It's Mother." He shook the receiver toward me.

I waved it away and sank down on a chair to remove my sandals. Rain blew in the open door.

"Idiot!" I snarled at Emmett and got up trailing water across the carpet to the door. I slammed it so hard that the outside shutters rattled.

"Sh-h. It's a bad connection," Emmett warned.

I looked at my watch to see if it was wet. Only four o'clock. That was strange. Something must be wrong if Earlene, who practiced all the small economies the rest of the family used, couldn't wait an hour for the rates to change.

"What's the matter?" I whispered.

Emmett shook his head. "Why do you need me there right now, Mother? Why don't you come down here if you're so lonesome? Aunt Bertha has plenty of room." He shrugged his shoulders at me.

"No. I'm downstairs. It's raining like hell. Celia just came in…all wet. I don't know where Aunt Bertha is, upstairs asleep maybe if the phone didn't wake her up, or if Celia didn't wake her beating on the doorbell. Maybe she's out playing bridge. I just got in a few minutes ago. Youall getting any rain up there?"

Emmett sat on the floor with his back to the wall listening and nodding as he looked up at the ceiling, the same way he would have listened if his mother were standing in front of him. He thumbed the closed pages of the telephone book.

I sneezed, picked up my sandals, and started upstairs. It was cold in the house, and I needed dry clothes. If anything was wrong Emmett would tell me. Earlene had probably called just to check on him. Bertha and I had reminded him to write his mother. Naturally he hadn't. Upstairs I found Bertha, fully dressed, sitting on the edge of her bed where she'd evidently been taking off her stockings. She cradled the receiver to her ear with one hand while covering up the mouthpiece with the other.

Trying to make enough noise to shame her into hanging up, I stood in front of the closet Emmett and I still shared and dropped my sandals. In a moment I looked around the opened door. Aunt Bertha hadn't attempted escape. She remained huddled on the edge of the bed with her ear pressed against the receiver and a worried expression on her face.

"Earlene," she broke in. "Listen. This is Bertha. I picked up the upstairs phone to make a call and heard you talking. Earlene, listen to me. This sort of thing happens all the time. I know. I know, and I'm sorry, but he doesn't have to— What?"

She appeared to be listening when she wasn't. She made up her mind about things and went right on thinking whatever she'd decided was right.

"Well, there are lots of things that can be done. There are ways— Earlene, I know you're upset, particularly since Estes is gone. All right. We'll talk about it later, but remember that isn't the only answer. Why don't you talk to Martha and Will.

They're bound to— Hush up, Emmett. This is the whole family's problem whether you like it or not! Earlene, don't worry. We'll work something out. I'll talk to you later. Give Will and Martha a call now. We can all talk more when Estes gets back. And Earlene, please— Calm down. Fix yourself a drink. I think I'll fix myself one." She repeated a string of admonitions before she hung up.

I could hear Emmett running upstairs. I met him at the top landing.

"What's wrong?"

He raised his hand and let it fall again on the banister's newel post.

"You don't know? You really don't know?" He looked at me closely and laughed. It was a mean dry laugh like the snort a horse gives when you're standing in front of him getting ready to bridle, and he's feeling impatient because he hates the bit and, at the same time, knows he's going to have to take it.

"Well, let me tell you . . . since everybody's telling me." Raising his voice, he leaned in the direction of the door to Aunt Bertha and Uncle Mowrey's room. "Nothing's wrong. These things happen all the time. Nothing in the world is wrong except Doris Lacey's pregnant, and Mama thinks we should get married right away."

Bertha came out to the landing buttoning her housedress as she walked. "You don't have to marry her, Emmett. Don't be a fool." She put her hand on his arm.

He pushed past both of us to the bedroom and slumped down on the side of his bed.

"You really don't have to marry her!" Bertha insisted. She turned and followed him.

I came behind her. We both stood at the foot of the twin bed that Emmett hadn't made. He sat on a pile of rumpled sheets refusing to look at either of us. The fan had been turned off. Rain dribbled down the long windowpanes.

"If she wants to have the baby," Bertha said, "there are places she can go, homes where she can stay till it's born. Then she can give it up for adoption. Plenty of girls do that . . . more than you'd think."

"I don't know. . . . Maybe Doris—"

"Well you don't have to decide right now."

"No."

"But you'd better be thinking about—"

"Aunt Bertha—" I looked at Emmett who appeared to be staring through the wet window to the house across the street, then I took Bertha's arm and whispered, "Better to leave him alone a little."

We left him to go back downstairs, Bertha leading. I knew it made no difference to Emmett whether plenty of people were in the same trouble or not. This was his trouble, and he had to take it in.

I was cold and wet. Water oozed down my neck from my wet hair. Grabbing a towel from the bathroom on the way down, I wrapped my head in it.

It had all happened so quickly . . . Earlene's hysterical call, Emmett's anger, at himself I guessed, at his mother, and at Bertha. And Doris? Was he angry at her too?

Uncle Estes, I discovered, was in Kansas checking on cattle he'd shipped to market, so Earlene hadn't talked to anybody else; maybe she hadn't even talked to him. She'd had to talk to someone. With the news of Doris's pregnancy, Earlene was like a small volcano at the point of eruption. Who had told her? Not Doris. I couldn't imagine Doris Lacey driving out to the ranch to tell Earlene anything. Her father Ed Lacy, I heard later, had appeared at Earlene's front door when she was home alone. He'd asked for Estes first, then for Emmett. Since they were both gone, he chose to talk to Earlene. Doris, he said, didn't know he was there.

Of course she had some pride. Why hadn't anybody considered that? Why hadn't they thought of Doris at all? Earlene and Bertha both acted as if she hardly existed, as if Emmett was the only one that mattered, Emmett and his future.

He'd acted that way himself at first. He didn't call Doris, wouldn't talk to Aunt Bertha except to borrow her car, and walked right past me without a word when he left the house.

Luis and I were sitting on the top step of his beach house talking and watching the moon rise. He'd been in Houston all day, he said, buying supplies, doing errands for his father and had come by the Mcleans' without calling. Why did I act as if I believed everything he told me? I needed to, wanted to. I couldn't ask him whose Austin-Healey had been there that afternoon. I had no right to push him against the wall with questions. Although Aunt Bertha asked him to stay for supper, we went to Gaido's to eat then drove out to his house.

Emmett swerved Bertha's Chrysler—evidently she'd relaxed her no-car rule—toward the steps, catching and holding Luis and me in its beams a long moment before turning off the lights. He walked slowly up the steps, the moonlight at his back. A few steps up he stumbled and muttered under his breath. As he got closer, I could smell whisky.

He grinned at both of us and, as usual, denied the obvious. "I'm not drunk."

"Where's your hat?" I asked.

"Left it with Jane."

"Where's Jane?"

"Down at Omar's drinking with Roby and Leslie and some other folks. That's what she likes . . . drinking."

Had he gotten her pregnant too? The question came to mind. What a mess that would be, Doris and Jane both pregnant. Not likely even if Jane would party all night. I'd met girls like her at the university. Liquor was a screen they used. Some of them acted as if they were drunker than they actually were. It was easy. You just kept adding water, or soda, or Coke. Nobody noticed. I did it myself at times, especially if I was going out with somebody I liked. It was safer that way. Jane wasn't playing safe though. She really drank, passed out, according to Emmett.

She could drink a lot. Once she started she always wanted to drink too much. What could you do with a girl who wasn't there? Liquor wasn't a screen for Jane. It was a magic potion that made her invisible.

Luis and Emmett were talking quietly. Luis pulled his car key out of his pocket. He carried a single key, one of the reasons he liked to coming back to Galveston. In Guanajuato he had to carry four or five because everything was locked . . . the door to the wall around the house, the house itself, the bodega—a storage room behind his house—his car, his studio.

Emmett laughed and said, "I can't take Aunt Bertha's car down to Post Office Street. Somebody might believe Uncle Mowrey's there."

I took Luis's dangling key from his hand. "You're too drunk—"

"Nah! Not me." He grabbed my hand, caught the key by the small leather strap Luis carried it on, and dropped it in his pocket.

Only half believing what was happening, I turned to Luis. "He doesn't know how to drive an MG."

"I can drive it. Friend of mine at school has one. It's only got one more gear than any other car."

I tried one more time. "Let us take you home."

He handed Luis the keys to Bertha's car. "We'll switch when you bring Celia in." He left us to lurch down the stairs.

I started to rise and follow him.

Luis caught my wrist. "Let him go. That's just what he'd like. He'd like for you to follow him. Why do you care where he goes?"

"He can go to all the whore houses in the world if that's what he wants. I don't care. But he's already too drunk to look after himself. He'll have a wreck, or get rolled—" I pulled my wrist free and sat down abruptly. I was doing it again, looking after Emmett like all the rest of the family's women. Beneath the house I could hear the car's motor start.

Luis watched me steadily. "I don't think he's that drunk. All the business about the car and somebody thinking your uncle was in one of the houses— That was just an excuse to come out here. He wants you to try to stop him. He probably won't even go down there. If he does, Celia, somebody will look after him. They're used to dealing with drunks, and if he's really as drunk as he's acting— They can't afford any rough stuff at the houses. Bad for business. There's always a bouncer around and a policeman not too far away." He smiled. "In fact Post Office is one of the quietest streets in Galveston."

"He's got that look on his face . . . that crazy grin."

"He'll be back," Luis said.

I watched him paint a thin coat of blue on a canvas. Specks of blue already covered the floor. Turpentine's clean stinging smell, linseed oil, paint, and steam from coffee together with a light wind coming in over the water rose and floated through the room. The bamboo shades had been rolled to the tops of the open windows. Against one wall was an old couch with an olive drab colored army footlocker at one end. I sat on it holding a coffee cup, my back to the L-shaped kitchen. To my right a doorway led to the bath and two bedrooms.

I looked over at the rusty tin cans still propped in a row on the table to a full length picture of Luis's brother Rico in his Marine dress uniform. Except for his height, they didn't look much alike. Or maybe pictures of young men in uniform generally showed them looking as determined and serious as Rico did, so they could scarcely look like themselves. They were marines, airmen, soldiers, sailors, men going off to war. I meant to ask Luis sometime if his brother favored his mother since he didn't seem to resemble his father, but I'd only seen Mr. Platon once, and the lights in the Balinese Room were dim. My brother looked like our mother's people, while I could see my father's in my long oval face. Emmett had his mother's dark hair. . . . And Emmett's and Doris's child . . . which side of the family would it look like? I hadn't told Luis about that. It was Emmett's problem, and I wouldn't question Luis about resemblance just then. He was working as if he'd forgotten me, Emmett, everyone.

Though I'd been in the studio before, I'd never seen him at work. Painting was something he did alone usually, and when he'd stopped to pick me up, he'd interrupted his schedule. Or perhaps it was already interrupted. Perhaps he really had been to Houston. At any rate he was only preparing canvas, covering one he'd already stretched with an undercoating. A bundle of paint smeared rags was loosely gathered on the table near his easel, and on the same table was a collection of mashed paint tubes, a dirty palette, brushes in an old pickle jar, a coffee can half full of turpentine. The space in front of him was clear. He'd taken down the topographical map and his mother's old gardening hat, a floppy yellowed straw. Facing him now was only the corner's triangle of weathered boards salvaged from old houses; others like them lined the whole room with gray and brown and traces of ingrained white. He slapped on more blue paint.

"It looks like fun."

"Other people's work usually does, doesn't it? If you want to try, I've got another easel and some boards. They have a texture a little like canvas."

"I . . . I don't know. I can't draw."

"Most of the painters I know had to learn how to. You have to learn how to see first. You have to keep looking. Then the hands, the muscles somehow begin to know what your eyes see. Here—"

He walked over to the kitchen, pulled out a tall stool, reached up to a shelf behind me, selected two clay pots, and put them on the stool. From a pile propped against the wall, he took a white board covered with something, some sort of fake canvas. Then he rummaged through drawers until he found a drawing pad. Tearing a sheet of paper off, he clipped the whole pad to the board. In a hall closet he found an extra easel and propped the board on it. He handed me a skinny black stick.

"Charcoal. Here's your first lesson. Draw those pots."

I'd never seen such a blank piece of paper, such a white,

empty rectangle. The longer I looked, the blanker and whiter it seemed. It was a whiteness that would show the smallest mark, a blankness that would surround a speck, and it waited on me to do something, to make something.

"The pots," I said. "They're . . . they're sort of dull."

"What do you want to draw?"

"I don't know . . . flowers maybe."

"Too complicated. Start with something simple." Luis hardly looked around to speak to me.

First I tried to draw the outline of each one. The charcoal was so soft I broke the stick immediately. When I tried to place the stool under the pots, it wouldn't come out right. Instead of a stool, there was only part of a circle. Nothing was in perspective. I could see that much. The paper was already smudged with lines I'd tried to erase with my fingers.

"Luis, how do you— These things are flat. I might as well have laid them down and traced around them."

"Look." He tore my sheet off, took the longer half of my charcoal, and made five lines with it. The circle was well on the way to becoming a stool. He handed the charcoal back to me. "Stare at the pots until you don't have to look at them. What makes them round, low, or high? Where is the light coming from? Search for the shadows. Try to draw the lines you know are there even if you can't see them."

I stared at the ochre yellow pots. Tentatively I sketched shadows, changed more lines. The pots still looked flat to me. I tore the sheet of drawing paper off the board, crumpled it, and let it fall to the floor. Another sheet followed, then a third and fourth. I glanced around Luis's shoulder to his canvas. He was adding blobs of rust colored paint to his blue canvas although he seemed to be scraping off more than he was putting on. Maybe it was more fun with paint. At least I'd have color then. I looked at the blank page and the dumb pots again and thought about how I needed to learn how to take news photos. I needed a course in press photography, and could probably take one the next semester.

"What's happening?" Luis asked quietly; most of his attention was still held by his canvas. He poked through the collection of stuff on the table beside him searching, perhaps, for a certain color among the half-empty paint tubes.

"Nothing. This demands a talent I don't have and a lot of patience. I might learn to draw in a hundred years, but I believe I'd be tired of these pots by then."

Lights, framed for a few seconds by the open windows, flashed past the house. Not many people drove on that part of the beach at night. I could hear a car's motor. Running out to the deck, I caught sight of the MG. Emmett hollered as he drove down the beach and made a wide looping turn.

"You were right. He's back," I called to Luis.

He kept on painting. "Yeah. Well, he'll find us."

Again I heard the car's motor. It was odd recognizing it above the sound of the surf. I thought of my parents waiting up for Kenyon late at night, how the colonel knew the sound of his old pickup's motor just before my brother turned into the driveway.

Emmett drove back in front of the house. One hand grabbing air like a bronc rider's he zig-zagged the car from beach to dunes to beach again. Moonlight outlined the pattern of his tracks.

"He's . . . he's— I guess he's drunker than ever."

Luis joined me at the deck rail. "He's going to get stuck. Hey, Emmett!" He shouted.

"What's he trying to do?" I stood at the rail trying to imagine where he would go next.

We could barely see the car beside a dune but could hear Emmett revving the motor and shouting like a rider coming out of a chute. As we watched, the car shot out headed straight to the water. This time he didn't cut back to the beach He drove straight into the Gulf yelling as he went.

I ran barefooted after Luis down the stairs and across the beach. Small waves fell against the car. Its motor dead, it rocked slowly almost floating. Emmett slumped forward over the steering wheel as if he were urging the MG on.

We waded in after him.

"He's all right. It's too shallow for him to drown," Luis shouted above the surf.

"That's good. I don't think he knows how to swim. Emmett, get out!" I screamed. Waves lapped my legs; though the water was only slightly cool, I was shaking.

"Watch out!" Luis warned from the opposite side of the car. "It could turn over."

I grabbed the top of the driver's door. "Are you all right?"

Emmett gazed silently out to sea as if he were dazed or dreaming.

"Luis, help me. I think he's knocked out." I felt his shoulder. It was wet, but warm as any living body's. "Maybe he's hurt inside."

"Nah!" Emmett snorted and looked at me as if he didn't quite know who I was.

"Well get out of there. What do you think you're doing?"

"Always wanted to see how far—" He grinned. "Wanted to see how far a fellow could take a car out on this sand." He laughed. Then with a drunk's quick mood change, he sighed.

A wave sprayed over the windshield. Drops ran down my arms and Emmett's face making him look like he could be crying even though he wasn't. He just sat there glaring at the wet windshield.

"Come on." Luis had waded around to my side and was standing next to me.

"Youall, let me be!" Emmett shouted.

I grabbed him by the shoulder again. "You're stuck, aren't you?"

"Tide's rising," Luis said. I could feel his legs in the water beside mine.

Emmett slowly pulled himself up out of the seat and tried to shift his body around while at the same time shoving the door open. He fell headfirst out of the side of the car into the oncoming waves.

We caught him under his arms and, with the help of the tide, pulled him to the beach.

"Wouldn't you know! He's got his damn boots on!" The wind plastered my wet shirt and shorts to my skin.

"Wait here. I'll get some blankets."

"Luis, your car—"

He shrugged and ran to the house leaving me sitting on the wet sand pushing Emmett's hair out of his face.

"Agaah!" He rolled his head away.

"Stupid!" I was so angry I felt I could spend a whole night calling him names.

"Yeah." Slowly he dragged his hand across his face. "I'm a worthless son-of-a-bitch."

"Sometimes."

He struggled to sit up, and when he'd managed to, stared toward the sea. Slowly he began pulling his boots off letting the water dribble on the sand while he held onto the heels shaking them.

"I don't know why . . . why she wouldn't tell me— Why in the hell she— Doris." He said her name in a wondering way. "Why wouldn't she tell me?"

I watched him emptying his boots, setting them straight up the way he put them in the closet when he was being careful.

"Maybe she didn't want to face anything. Maybe she's mad at you. I bet you haven't written her a word. She probably guessed you were sent down here. Doris isn't dumb, you know."

"She ought to have told me."

"That's your idea, not hers."

"She's a good little old girl." He peeled off his socks and threw them toward the incoming tide.

I could still smell whisky on him—bourbon mixed with sea water—though now he seemed sober.

Luis had come back with an armload of old army blankets.

Whenever I saw them I thought of the ones my father had brought home. They were everywhere. Most of the world could have been covered with olive drab wool.

We wrapped ourselves up in the blankets, and all three of us sat on the beach watching the waves pushing against the MG as if we were the three wise monkeys cast in bronze, unhearing, unseeing, unspeaking. The waves kept battering at the car's small, rakish frame. Moonlight bounced off its windshield. We were so quiet we could have been admiring the view.

Emmett got up, walked over to the Chrysler and found a chain in the trunk. I remained huddled in my blanket. Luis took the chain from him, carried it to his car, and attached it to the rear bumper. They did this almost automatically, walking back and forth without saying a word to each other. Emmett, at the wheel of the other car, pulled the MG to safety. All three of us stood in a line silently watching saltwater slide down the sides and over the fenders to disappear in the sand. I wondered if little specks of salt would show when the car dried.

"If you can get it fixed, Luis, I'll pay for it," Emmett said.

Luis looked over at him for a long moment. "Yeah."

How much did that car still matter to him? It had been his mother's. He drove it every summer when he came up from Mexico to visit his father. I was almost sure it couldn't be fixed. Salt air wore Galveston cars away. Uncle Mowrey had talked about bicycles, apparently in perfect order after the 1900 storm, falling to pieces when they dried out. The old MG had been half submerged in salt water.

Early the next morning Emmett, without asking anyone's help, arranged for Luis's car to be towed to a garage. Around nine I went with him to the place where a mechanic was already bent over another car's open hood when we drove up. On the opposite side of the building I could see the MG looking quite dry as if it had never been soaked in the Gulf. Full of tools and automobiles, the shop had a greasy metallic smell; a dangling light bulb showed its blackened floor.

I leaned against Aunt Bertha's car waiting in the morning sun while Emmett walked into the cave of the garage and got the attention of the half hidden mechanic.

When they had finished talking Emmett, with a disgusted look and one wave of his arm, motioned for me to get back in the car. He walked slowly looking down at the ground, pulled the door open, got in, and stared out the windshield blankly for a moment.

Still looking straight ahead, he said, "This guy says they could clean it up, strip all the upholstery out, replace it, and coat all the metal parts with oil, but something would always go wrong. His idea is for me to take it off the island and sell it to someone else on the mainland, pass it off as used maybe once it's cleaned up. I don't know what kind of crook he thinks I am. I want the damn thing fixed." He looked over toward the little car before we pulled out to the street.

I had always thought if you totaled something, the insurance would be enough to pay for a new one, but Uncle Mowrey, trying not to smile, told me that morning you only get the price the old car would bring. For all my ignorance about insurance, I was sure Luis wouldn't be paid enough to replace it. So was Emmett.

"You know Luis wouldn't want a new MG, Emmett. Maybe you could find another old one."

"No. . . . That old one he had was the one he wanted. Anyway, Celia, you don't know much about cars. Cars like that— The older they are, the harder they are to find. And that one is nearly a antique." He kept his eyes on the traffic flowing by the sea wall. It was one of those Saturdays when it seemed everybody on the mainland had decided to go to the beach.

"I guess I better go tell him," he said.

We drove out to Luis's house. It was almost noon by then, and from the deck I could see the harsh sun shining on Emmett's tire tracks carved in the sand the night before; some of them were high enough to have escaped the tide's reach.

Luis was laconic about his loss. "It was about to fall apart anyway," he said.

"I'm sorry," said Emmett. He was morose by that time.

"I can use my father's until I leave. It's stored in the Galvez garage. Every Sunday I take it out, take my father and his car for a drive."

Emmett groaned and sat down on the steps with his chin in his hand. "I totaled your car, and I—" He looked up at Luis. "How can I do anything—?"

He seemed more worried about Luis's car than Doris Lacey's pregnancy at that point. One worry displaced another maybe, shifted attention from the uncertain future to the certain present. In the end Mr. Platon's insurance company paid him a small sum for the old MG, and Emmett borrowed money from his father to add to that. Guilt money, I thought, but I didn't mention it to Emmett. By then there was no need to.

Chapter Eleven

When her mother called her to come to the phone, Doris Lacey hung up the minute Emmett said her name.

He stomped out of the room to the back porch and began pacing it. After a few minutes, he banged the yard's gate closed then evidently changed his mind, as he wheeled around, swung the gate open, and came back inside.

When he started toward the phone again, I shook my head.

"Well, how am I going to get her to talk to me?"

"Emmett, do you think all you have to do is to say 'toad' and she'll hop?"

"This baby—"

"It isn't with us yet. Maybe she's decided to do something else. Maybe she called those people, the ones at the home Aunt Bertha was talking about."

"I don't think Doris would do that."

"Maybe it isn't even your baby."

"Celia! She's my girl! If it's anybody else's baby, how come her daddy was talking to my mama?"

"I bet you she didn't know he was going to."

"Well, what if she didn't?"

We weren't getting anywhere, so I suggested his real problem might be guessing what she had in mind.

"Yeah. Well how do I do that?"

He chewed his bottom lip and looked at me as if I might be refusing to tell him what he most needed to know. The only thing I knew was Emmett had to discover Doris's needs himself.

We'd disagreed with each other daily, but for the first time, we both tried to work something out. That afternoon he sent Doris a postcard with a picture of the Gulf on front—too blue, stretching out to nowhere. Before going out to mail it, he flashed it in front of me. On it he'd written, "I'll be home on the 2:30 train Thursday."

Though I'd wished his message had been longer and I'd hoped he might send her a letter, the card was Emmett's style. Now he'd have to go back to Mullin, back to the dusty little settlement near the ranch, and I would have to go too. We had been in Galveston almost a month, nearly as long as our parents had planned, and it was just as well since Aunt Bertha wasn't sleeping any better at the end of our stay than I had been at the beginning.

After I looked at Emmett's card, I told him he might as well ask to be met by a brass band because the postman on the Lacey's route would, in his neighborly way, undoubtedly spread the word. What was more, people in Mullin might even guess exactly why he was coming. He knew as well as I about the way everyone loved to jump to conclusions.

"Fine with me," he said. "Maybe she'll speak to me when I get there. She might as well, don't you think? If we're going to get married—"

"Emmett, what if she won't?"

He looked at me as if I'd asked him something so fundamentally dumb he might ignore the question. "She may not want to," I added. I didn't think he'd even considered such a possibility.

"It's my baby!"

"It's hers too. It's her life."

He gave me another long look and stalked off to the mailbox like a man overlooking a small pebble he'd just stumbled across in the street.

Whatever Ed Lacey had said to Aunt Earlene, I still didn't think he'd told Doris before he went. Or maybe his wishes didn't carry the same weight with his daughter. It was a sad plan for a shotgun wedding, a demanding father and a reluctant bride, the same result I'd so often dreaded.

Luis laughed at my assumptions and suggested that Doris simply didn't want anyone to know it was a shotgun wedding.

I wasn't sure. Doris was pretty straightforward. She might really not want to marry Emmett. I was sure she hadn't been interested in him just for the sake of the ranch. If she was simply greedy, there were other boys around who'd inherit land in counties nearby. She could have known some of them. I never thought Doris or her parents—for that matter—were so conniving. Aunt Earlene's exaggerated notions of the importance of her own social standing led her to make foolish accusations. Doris would marry someone she loved, and I desperately wanted to believe she still had a choice.

"It's hard to tell who does the choosing sometimes, isn't it?" I said to Luis. "Maybe they both choose and they don't know it."

He looked puzzled for a moment then shook his head, "I think one of the two always knows, Celia."

He'd dropped by the Mcleans' late in the morning for coffee. Bertha had been working her way through a long list of ingredients in a gumbo recipe and seemed pleased to see him. They discussed the merits of browning fresh versus frozen okra until I thought I might go out and wait on the steps. In the middle of comparisons of Louisiana and Texas gumbos, Aunt Bertha, in her usual abrupt way, interrupted to ask about his father.

"He's . . ." He paused as if he were having second thoughts. "You haven't heard?"

Bertha flicked the heat down under the gumbo, moved the coffeepot to the kitchen table, and turned back to him slowly.

"He and Louise Finley. They're going to marry."

"Really?" I could hear my Tennessee aunts', my grandmothers,' my mother's voices, a chorus of women dissembling, speaking in the same expression of polite disbelief. There was nothing in her tone implying either pleasure or regret. I knew she thought Mr. Platon should remarry. As far as Luis could tell though, she was only receiving information. Then she added, "She'll be a good companion for him."

"You think so?" Luis asked as if he were merely inquiring.

"Oh, I actually don't know her that well, but at least he won't be so lonely any more." She poured more coffee, led us to the back porch where she promised to join us—her usual method for getting people out of the kitchen so she could concentrate—and left us sitting there.

Luis stretched his legs out in front of him, stared at the small yard where the red and yellow hibiscus were still in bloom and sighed as if he couldn't stand the sight of them.

He looked so unhappy I said, "Maybe it's only strange at first. Later you'll—"

"I doubt once I'm used to the idea I'll like it. I doubt I'll ever get used to it and even if I do...." He shook his head.

Emmett and I took a morning train from Galveston. Aunt Bertha, Uncle Mowrey, and Luis came down to the station to see us off. Emmett and Aunt Bertha withdrew to argue quietly, Bertha doing most of the talking. She wouldn't give up her arguments against his marrying. Most of all, she was sure he was too young. She was also afraid of an early divorce. Emmett nodded now and then politely, not really hearing. He was as good at this sort of pretense as he was about slipping out of a house quickly without anyone noticing. Beginning with his mother, he'd been practicing all his life on ways to avoid bossy women.

For a while Uncle Mowrey paced between two posts; after watching them from a little distance for a while, he walked over to take Aunt Bertha by one arm, Emmett by the other.

Beyond them the Santa Fe, steaming and hissing, glistened in the sun while Luis and I waited further down on the platform beside a high flatbed wagon heaped with gray canvas bags labeled U. S. MAIL. From now on the mail would carry my letters back to Galveston just as it had carried my letters to Tony, to friends, to my parents in Leon. I was continually saying good-bye to one set of people, and hello to another. There would be someone else to write now, Luis in Galveston or in Mexico.

He wished I could stay longer, he said, and I believed him; both of us were adrift that summer. I reminded him he was older, freer to come and go, especially since his father had decided to remarry. My parents wanted me to come home, and I still had to do as they wished.

The porter emerged from the car ahead of us. While talking to Luis, I watched him place the shiny metal auxiliary step in front of those leading to the train, then he picked up Emmett's and my suitcases and carried them inside. After wearing only shirts, shorts and sandals all day for weeks I felt uncomfortably bound by my dress, stockings and heels.

At the moment of our leave-taking, there was a silvery flash of metal step, behind it was the larger flash of the passenger car; the smell of steam and diesel mingled in Galveston's humid morning air. And there was an indefinable sadness, one I knew from all the other times I'd left places no matter how old I was, no matter whether I'd liked it or hated it. Emmett called my name. Aunt Bertha beckoned to me. I turned to Luis and knew then, knew by the slightly formal way he hugged me, that he preferred men. I'd probably known it for sometime. This came to me so definitely that I searched his face for a moment as if to memorize it and to remember that this entirely desirable man always would love and be loved by other men.

Emmett and I sat on the scratchy seats side by side and waved to our aunt and uncle. Luis waited behind them a little.

"You seeing him again?" he asked.

"He says he'll come up to Austin this fall."

"He's queer, you know."

I nodded. Emmett had seen him in a bar one afternoon with a boy. They hadn't come in together but they left together.

"I don't know what it was about them. They just looked at each other a certain way maybe. They drove off in an Austin Healey."

"Red?"

"Yeah. But if you knew—? Why did you keep on seeing him?"

"I like him. He's good company."

He shook his head. "I didn't figure him out for a while myself. I don't guess Aunt Bertha knows. Once that woman gets a notion about anything. . . ." He threw his head back as if shaking off all her arguments, "I'm going to get married!"

"Emmett, where's your hat?"

"Gave it to Jane." He grinned.

We crossed the neck of the bay sliding by the old causeway as we passed it on the new one and were on the mainland once more. The train picked up speed. Other passengers, steadying themselves by holding onto the tops of seats as they swayed in the aisle, smiled down on us benevolently like we were a pair of newlyweds on our way home from our honeymoon. I would have minded when we rode down to Galveston. It made no difference now.

Later that afternoon while the sun scorched the drought bitten fields and the air-conditioned train wound its way northwest through transparent waves of heat, he went to sleep at last. His head rolled from side to side on the white square of cotton covering the seat's back. I pulled him toward my shoulder. By the time we hit the next to last stop, he woke up and rubbed his eyes. Taking my hand, he turned it palm up, studied it for a little, then let go. His eyes flickered shut again.

"Better wake up. They'll be there when we get in."

When he opened his eyes once more, he looked at me as if we'd met in a dream, and he didn't quite know who I was yet, as if he'd been dreaming of some time long before we'd ever gone to Galveston.

"What? Who?" He shook his head. A white line showed above his collar where the barber had trimmed away his dark hair. The first haircut he'd had all summer left him looking vulnerable. He was twenty, going on twenty-one, and for the moment, tamed.

"My mother and yours. They said they would meet us."

"Christ!"

"Don't you remember?"

"Well, yes, but I want to see Doris first. I wish we could go right on to California or wherever the hell this train goes. And I know we can't. Mama's going to tie into me." He looked out the window. "Country's gone to hell. We haven't passed over a river with water enough to matter. I've been looking at the ocean so long I nearly forgot about the damn drought."

Like all the Chandlers, he talked about the weather when he wanted to evade a touchy subject. I'd thought he was determined to marry. Maybe he was only trying to talk himself into it. What was a baby to him after all? The world was full of young girls and their bastard children. There were whole institutions devoted to them, a place in Austin, a Catholic home near the hospital west of campus, and another one in Ft. Worth where unmarried pregnant girls were sheltered. I'd walked by the one in Austin plenty of times and wondered what those girls' lives were like. I supposed those were the homes Aunt Bertha had talked about, and there were others, no doubt. If they chose to, the girls could give their babies up to some well-educated, financially able couple dying for a child.

By this time though I'd begun to believe Doris Lacey wouldn't choose to give up her child. She was a country girl still, and a senior in Mullin's small high school, but she was bright and spirited. Emmett swore she was bent on college even if she had to wait tables. She'd been riding in the barrel races for several years when Emmett took up bronc riding. I'd asked her once what she thought of his riding. She'd laughed and said he might learn how to stick to something, and if he couldn't, he'd learn how to fall off. His family could worry about his safety. Doris narrowed her gaze, watched him ride and took him to the doctor who wrapped his chest when he cracked a rib. She wasn't a person who wasted time wringing her hands.

"Emmett, I can't really imagine Doris giving up her baby. On the other hand, she could just go away somewhere, stay with a relative and have it."

"In secret?"

"Oh Lord, Emmett! Women must have been doing that forever!"

"Maybe. I don't know. I have to see Doris. I want to see her. It's Mother. She's always said I'd get somebody pregnant, or break my neck riding, or wake up in jail, and there'd be hell to pay."

His summing up of Aunt Earlene's assessment of him didn't sound quite like her. It was a little raw. Maybe those were the fates that Emmett had warned himself against.

The train slid to a stop at the familiar red brick depot. My mother and Aunt Earlene were waiting in the shade of the doorway. I waved at them. They didn't see me at first. Aunt Earlene craned her neck looking for Emmett everywhere. He was right behind me bumping our suitcases against the seats.

When we emerged from the train a smothering blanket of heat fell over us. I had the same impulse Emmett had earlier. If only we could have gone on and on and never gotten off, never come back, never come back to all the life that was waiting for us there, back to Kenyon's problems, to my father's impatience, to the little heap of worries families seemed to accumulate. All of these were underlined by the persistent Texas summer which wouldn't let up till sometime late in October. Inland heat was a force I always wanted to escape. It was only slightly cooler in Galveston, however we generally had a sea breeze. In Leon air-conditioning was the only relief. Though we had some in church, there were no high ceilinged rooms with fans in anyone's house in town. Except for some of the buildings around the square, the courthouse, the remnants of a log jail and three or four houses, there was nothing particularly old in town. My parents had brought me there. The university had already taken me away. I'd gradually left little by little, semester by semester. I'd been going to Tennessee, to Colorado, to Mexico and coming back every summer. The impulse to go on was only that of someone who hasn't finished traveling. I would take it up again later.

Aunt Earlene swooped toward Emmett with her arms out-stretched like a great hovering bird waiting to enfold him.

Emmett bent his head to kiss her cheek.

My mother kissed me then stepped back, "You look like two gypsies. You must have lived in the water. Did you have a good time?"

I was immensely grateful she didn't ask about Tony Gregory. After a while I would tell her; she knew this wasn't the right time.

She was wearing a green and white checked dress with a short sleeved green jacket that she often wore on shopping trips to Waco. If she went anywhere with Earlene, their unspoken rivalry compelled her to dress up.

Aunt Earlene hugged me and said, "I'm so glad you're back." She had on a spicy smelling perfume and a beautifully tailored brown linen dress. As usual she could have been in downtown Dallas.

Emmett rolled his eyes skyward.

The train clanked noisily, wheezed steam, and surged away. No one had gotten aboard.

We'd come home. The comforting banalities waited. Yes, Uncle Estes was back from Kansas. Of course it hadn't rained a drop. They had drilled two new water wells at the ranch. My brother, Kenyon, had started a job as a cowboy at the livestock auction barn just west of Leon. He would be busy, Mother told me, driving livestock from the unloading corral to holding pens to the arena and doing the whole thing again in reverse.

It would be dusty and could be dangerous. Kenyon was going to have to deal with a lot of stubborn, often frustrat-ing animals. He'd probably have to help feed and doctor too. The list of his duties seemed to please her, so I assumed we wouldn't have to worry much about Kenyon for a while. This didn't mean we were relieved of worry forever. Kenyon wasn't grown yet. It took him years. I changed careers, became a nurse, married a doctor, and had two children before he left home.

Wasn't it hot! Mother said it. Somebody had to. None of us ever got tired of complaining about the heat. Walking through the station's open doors, I scanned the parking lot for the Laceys' pickup. It wasn't there. Mother kept talking about how many days of over a hundred degrees weather they had endured. I glanced back at Emmett and heard him say he needed the car. Earlene started to speak, looked like she'd swallowed something that went down wrong, and stopped herself.

"Can't Aunt Martha carry you home, Mother?"

Mother and Aunt Earlene both acquiesced quickly even though it meant Mother would drive to Mullin and back, a hundred-mile trip by the time she got to the ranch, and forty more to get back to Leon, a drive she swore she wouldn't mind. I admired their willingness. Both of them knew where Emmett was going, and as different as they were, Mother and Aunt Earlene were determined to be helpful. I'd noticed this before; I understood their resolve now.

Emmett threw a suitcase in the trunk of each car. He got in his, started the motor and punched the button automatically rolling the windows up, sealing in the air-conditioning, sealing himself away from us in his mother's tan Buick which was almost the same color as the caliche topped country roads. I was sealed in also with Mother and Earlene both sitting up front. Earlene stared at the place where her car had been parked as if she couldn't quite believe Emmett had already come and gone. Cool air whooshed through the car. Transported from train to car like perishable vegetables being shifted from one refrigerated place to the next, Emmett and I had traveled through a third of Texas like a couple of heads of lettuce without knowing how the wind smelled, and if we had, we would have been exhausted by the heat. The contrariness of desires—Emmett no longer needing me just as I was beginning to enjoy him, the wish to be in Galveston as well as knowing we had to come home—struck me so that I sighed aloud.

Mother asked, "Well?"

And Aunt Earlene asked, "What has he done now?"

Since her question was easier, I said, "He sent Doris a post-card saying he'd be in today."

Small red spots appeared on her cheeks. "You mean to tell me he actually wrote to her?"

"Yes."

"Oh . . . well!" Earlene tried to smile, but her lips were so pursed together it fizzled out. "Martha, did you ever get a post-card from Emmett?"

Mother shook her head. "I hardly know what his hand-writing looks like, or Kenyon's either for that matter."

"He still has to ask Doris, Aunt Earlene. He just didn't want anybody telling him he had to."

"I already told him!" Earlene snapped. The red spots spread across her cheeks.

Mother drove quickly out of Temple. After we'd gone through Leon and reached the highway toward Mullin, Earlene relaxed a bit and began telling us about wedding plans.

She and Mother were debating about alcoholic and non-alcoholic punch when I decided to take off my stockings. I unhooked my garter belt, pulled it off, and peeled off the nylons. Then I stretched out on the back seat. There was noth-ing to hold anybody's attention on the road to Mullin, nothing to look at except yellowed dried pasture land, tired trees and, infrequently, a small white frame house set back from the road a little. On the whole it looked like lonesome country to me, a place no one would want to come to unless they had lived there always or owned land. I was bound for cities. The country around Leon and Mullin held no charms for me. Just looking at it made me thirsty.

I was nearly asleep when Earlene snagged on the question of allowing any alcohol at all.

"I don't think Estes would like a dry wedding."

Mother said she was sure my father wouldn't.

This problem kept Earlene occupied until we got to the ranch house where we found the driveway crowded with painters' trucks. Uncle Estes appeared from behind one of them looking more than ever like an aging movie star—his wheat-colored hair just beginning to gray—walking off the set to welcome his fans.

"I'm having the interior walls painted," Earlene explained as we picked our way around ladders and buckets.

The cement sidewalk was too hot for my bare feet. I had to run to the porch.

They had started painting over the living room walls and when it was finished the rest of the rooms looked too shabby to Earlene, so all of them had to be done.

"Of course Estes thinks I'm crazy, but it had to be painted sometime, and with a wedding coming on—"

Estes patted her on the back and said it was all right with him. He let her do what she pleased and seemed to enjoy the results. If he'd returned to find the house burned down, he would have surveyed the blackened remains and said, "Well, I guess we'll have to build another one," and they would have. He was a natural builder. Beginning with his father's small ranch, he'd expanded to others. Estes spent weeks on the road selling cattle in Kansas, checking on stock, and overseeing ranches he'd leased in South Texas, Colorado, and New Mexico. Someday all this would be Emmett's. Someday he would, if Earlene got her way, be like his father all over again only better. She'd already lost. Emmett was made of different stuff and he still had a lot of wildness to wear out.

When we were on the road back to Leon I finally asked, "What's the matter with Earlene? She talks about a wedding like she's the mother of the bride instead of the groom. You know as well as I do, as well as Earlene does, that the bride's family throws the reception. Won't the Laceys, if Doris will marry him, have to decide on stuff like alcohol in the punch?"

"Oh Celia, making plans for everybody helps keep her busy, and she needs to be busy just now. For her, I think, everything's fallen apart. She's trying to paste it all together again."

"But if they marry—"

"Celia, what do you mean 'if'?" Mother spoke as if it wasn't really a question, as if she too thought Emmett should marry.

"Doris wouldn't talk to Emmett. She's . . . I don't know exactly— Proud, I guess. Maybe she doesn't intend to marry or to keep the baby. Aunt Bertha thinks she should go to a home and—"

"Isn't that just like Bertha! She's lived in Galveston too long, forgotten what it's like up here, forgotten how people think about things. The Laceys will want Doris to marry Emmett."

"All right, Mother. Suppose they do. They still might want to make a few plans of their own. Or maybe Doris and Emmett would like to get married quietly by a J. P."

"Promise me, Celia, you won't even mention that possibility to Earlene. She's simply got to have this wedding!"

I made the promise, and it was an easy one to keep. Emmett didn't come home that night. He picked up Doris and drove to the border in his mother's car. They were married in Laredo. He sent his parents a wire from Mexico. "Doris and I married last night. Uncle Blanton and Alex witnessed. In Monterey. Be here a week."

It was like him not to have invited Aunt Ellen and Marie. They probably would have wanted to change their clothes for the ceremony, and he wouldn't wait. Or perhaps Aunt Ellen would have called his mother. By the time I saw the wire, it was all crumpled up. Earlene, angry, almost hysterical, had Estes drive her into Leon so she could show it to us.

Uncle Estes only grinned and said, "I never could imagine Emmett in a big church wedding." By then, Earlene had started the painters to work on the outside of their house. She needed a change, Estes decided, and took her off to the Colorado ranch for awhile.

Aunt Bertha's fears were unrealized. The marriage lasted. Doris and Emmett had a daughter and two sons. We see them seldom, especially since they moved to one of the ranches in New Mexico while my husband and I live in San Antonio.

Chapter Twelve

I climbed back into my car. All morning I'd been drifting about the neighborhood around the Mclean house as I had when I was there in fifty-three. I'd walked to the seawall and back and around many blocks nearby, straying almost as far as the library. Now, sitting in front of the house, I remember that I've lived in many houses before and since. And I've returned to look at several only to discover again it's merely momentary nostalgia that makes anyone wish either places or people would remain the same.

After I left the island that summer I changed careers twice, studied nursing, finished college, became a teacher briefly, moved to San Antonio. In the summers between, Leslie and I traveled to England and France and Italy. Later Edward Greenlee, the doctor I married in fifty-six, and I went back to France, on to Spain, and to Russia when the cold war was over. After our son and daughter were born, we rented houses abroad, old places in old countries, and made our journeys to them on foreign streets with names we had to learn how to pronounce, a contrast to the alphabetically named streets of the older part of Galveston.

I'd located the house intuitively. Now, for the first time, looking up at the street sign on the corner, I realized it was different. The whole area had become a historic district, and when it did, the name of the Mclean's street evidently was changed to an earlier one. How odd to realize a part of a personal past, a familiar loved place, has become public history.

It was time, I saw on the car's clock, to go back to the house where Luis lay dying of the disease he would barely name that was nonetheless evident in his emaciated body.

He'd gone to Edward for diagnosis and Edward had told him, then came home to tell me. "It's AIDS. He doesn't want to know it."

"He's not going to want us to do anything either."

Edward nodded.

"We could look after him here."

We have a comfortable house with empty bedrooms on a quiet street in San Antonio. Our children are grown and gone, but Luis would not come and stay with us, so I tried another way, knowing it was foolish, knowing I still wanted to make the offer.

"We could take you to Paris. I could go with you if you like. Edward could join us for awhile. You've always wanted to go, and it's so beautiful."

Too thin already, having problems with his eyes, he smiled and refused. He wouldn't go back to Mexico either. He'd kept the beach house in Galveston.

"I don't know how many hurricanes it has weathered."

He knew a doctor there. His friend Felipe would look after him.

"In Galveston it doesn't matter. So many of the people I knew there are dead already. People with . . . with this . . . don't live in Mexico."

He said it so wearily I knew he'd made up his mind much earlier to come back home to die. Ironically AZT was so much cheaper in Mexico. His friends there would supply him. He had a little money, just what he'd saved, and his inheritance from his father who left him the beach house.

Luis hadn't been back to Galveston but once or twice since his father died. He never liked his stepmother. However Louise Finley did keep his father company; a few weeks before she and Mr. Platon married he moved out of the hotel into her apartment. Later they bought one of the new condominiums just being built on the island. Somehow she got him to give up gambling. Still Luis wouldn't like her. No matter what she did, he found fault. Louise was one of those women who had never learned how to cook. The first time Luis visited them after they married he was enraged to discover Alberto eating crackers and cottage cheese at odd hours. She'd waited until she quit working to travel, so she and Alberto were frequently gone on long cruises. Aunt Bertha and Uncle Mowrey were once on the same ship with them to Hong Kong.

"Afloat in a sea of champagne dotted with islands of caviar," Luis commented.

Although his father had lived like a wastrel for almost three years, and Luis hadn't cared in the least, he was contemptuous of any sign of luxury in Louise's and Alberto's lives. His usual tolerance deserted him. He couldn't trust Louise. He didn't want another mother.

I thought Alberto knew this, for he made him executor of his will, a way of letting Luis know what happened to his estate. As usual he didn't seem to care though he admitted he needed money as much as anyone.

Louise Finley was left the condo and a small trust fund, which went to Luis when she died. Beside receiving the beach house, he inherited the duty of taking care of his father's bequests. Alberto left a number of small personal gifts to various people. One was a pair of gold cufflinks, which were to be given to Frank, the doorman at the Balinese Club.

"I looked all over town for him, or for someone who knew him, but he couldn't be found," Luis told me.

By the time Alberto died, Galveston had become a different city.

Driving to Luis's I watched a storm gathering over the Gulf. Gray clouds choked the sky. Waves rose high and fell greedily sucking at what was left of the sand, reaching over the granite boulders piled at the foot of the wall. Built to protect Galveston, the seawall blocked the natural action of waves against the island. The ramp we used to drive down to reach West Beach now dropped directly into water. The city has been saved, but the beach eroded daily, more obvious just before a storm when the wind driven waves rise against the wall. Sea and sand became a choppy mass broken only by red flags violently whipping on poles at the ends of drowned jetties. The wind carried seaweed's sharp medicinal smell. Far out, close to the horizon, a thread of lightning dangled against the gray sky.

Uncle Mowrey would have hated watching the beach erode. He had known it was happening; at least he didn't have to witness the result. Late in his life, after retirement, he and Bertha began to leave the island together to travel to warm countries. They took a long cruise to Hong Kong, shorter ones to the Caribbean and the West Indies. They came back, not to Galveston—too damp for their bones—but to San Antonio, to an apartment there. Bertha was through with houses. The Scottish sea captain's house Uncle Mowrey's father built was first rented, then willed to Bertha when Mowrey died, willed to Mowrey's distant cousin when Bertha died, sold finally to someone who cut it up into apartments, tore down the prim iron fence Emmett had caught his boot on, built the steps of raw boards, painted the shutters that nasty mustard yellow, covered the boards and battens with shingles, then left it all to be peeled by wind and rain.

Emmett never took the staircase put together with pegs that Aunt Bertha promised him. She made no mention of it in her will which was just as well; there was no place for it in a ranch house, and I doubt he would have taken the only staircase from a two story house. I smiled remembering its dark wood and narrow treads and how we seemed to be running up and down those steps all month. Standing on the deck of Luis's beach house, I watched the storm come in. A curtain of rain swept slowly over the sea toward the island.

Edward accepted Luis as he did the rest of my family. He was godfather to both our children. We went to his gallery openings in Mexico City, in Houston and in San Antonio.

For the past five or six years he'd brought Felipe with him when he came up from Mexico. Younger, handsome, no trace of effeminacy about him either, I saw Felipe as part of a familiar pattern, the boy who needed an older man. I thought he might be an artist also but no, he had an antique shop in Guanajuato and another in Mexico City. Sometimes Luis teased him a little about being a faker, for in Mexico there were factories full of craftsmen reusing old wood in old looking furniture.

"Recycling," Felipe said. "We have been doing it for years. You Americans are late in this game."

His English was excellent, much better than my Spanish has ever become.

"I'm sure we have our own fakers," I told him. I liked Felipe. Other boys had come to San Antonio with Luis. It appeared this one might stay. He had the quickness, the intuitiveness necessary.

In returning to Galveston, they came back to a tourist town. The Balinese Club, the Galveston equivalent of The Stork Club or El Trocadero, had been the city's little Monte Carlo on the Gulf, its shining palace of the night. Vaguely naughty, always exclusive, it has vanished. When Galveston was cleaned up in the late fifties and all the slot machines tossed into the bay, the Balinese Club was closed along with all the smaller clubs lining Seawall Boulevard. It was used as a nightclub and dinner theater, then sold, and closed again. At the west end of the island a bridge was built sometime in the sixties, a great arc that spans San Luis Pass and takes traffic on down to other beach settlements past Surfside to Freeport. Now West Beach is littered with piles of houses and condominiums.

Downtown the opera house, already a ruin in the fifties, has been reclaimed; its new grandeur may outshine the old. There are no whorehouses on Post Office Street. The sleazy little clubs have been replaced by sleazy bathing suit and T-shirt shops. On the seawall Cal's place has been taken by a series of guitar players. Like him, no doubt, they come and go with the summer crowds. There are other new museums, one for trains, one that mimics a rain forest. The library is larger. The refurbished Galvez has new owners and an intricate new pool. Many of the Victorian houses I saw in the historic district were saved. Some have been restored while others, like the Mcleans' house, quietly fall apart.

When Edward and I took the children to the beach one summer we heard a cabdriver say, "Galveston's too clean now."

We smiled at each other. His complaint was only an echo of the one Aunt Bertha and Uncle Mowrey used to make to visitors who were charmed by sun and sea and their tales of the wicked past

Galveston holds on and lets go, adapts and survives.

At Luis's I remained near his deck's front rail. The rain had blown in another direction. Edward wouldn't have to drive through it on his way down for the weekend. Other than Felipe, the two of us, and Leslie, who had married and lived on the island still, there was no one who knew Luis had chosen to return.

That he would not say the name of his disease didn't bother Edward, nor eventually, did his refusal seem incongruous to me. Discretion marked his whole life. Sometimes I wished he'd had the freedom to make himself known, but those who were his friends knew. There was no one to reject him, no one in Galveston save Leslie, and she hasn't. He wasn't shocked by imminent death; he has never thought of himself as invulnerable. Of course he wished for a longer time. He has liked his life, I suppose, as much as anyone does. Luis has lived with a certain style, and he has no intention of talking about his coming end to anyone, not to Edward or me, not to Felipe. He may have terrible fears, huge angers. I don't press him to reveal them, nor does he seem to want to. It is hard, some days, not to rage aloud. So we mourn him already among ourselves while he continues, according to his code, to be a proper man.

I left my seat on the deck and started inside to tell him what a wreck the Mclean house had become, then checked myself. What difference did the ruin of one old house make to a dying man? Better to tell him that the palm tree still lived although the house had been made into apartments and leave it at that. Restoration and ruin were both still evident in Galveston. Even if the natural balance between sea and sand had been destroyed by the seawall—Luis had noticed much of the beach was washed away—the old Christmas trees thrown on West Beach each year were catching sand which might, one day, pile higher and form dunes. And I could also tell him the ferry still ran its curved route to Bolivar directed by the currents, the tides and the winds, forces which would continue to rule all the earth's moving shifting ways.

About the Author

Carolyn Osborn graduated from the University of Texas at Austin with a B.J. degree in 1955, and an M.A. in 1959. She has won awards from P.E.N., the Texas Institute of Letters, and a Distinguished Prose Award from *The Antioch Review* (2003). Her stories have been included in *The O. Henry Awards* (Doubleday, 1991) and *Lone Star Literature* (Norton, 2003), among numerous other anthologies. She is the author of several collections of short stories, including: *A Horse of Another Color* (University of Illinois Press, 1977), *The Fields of Memory* (Shearer Publishing, 1984), and *Warriors & Maidens* (Texas Christian University Press, 1991). The Book Club of Texas published an illustrated, specially bound edition of her story, *The Grands* (1990). In 2009, she received the Lon Tinkle Award from the Texas Institute of Letters.

Acknowledgments

I am grateful for historical information from Gary Cartwright's *Galveston: A History of the Island* (1991) and from David G. McComb's *Galveston: A History* (1986).

For insight, my thanks go to Ann Dunlap, who was, from the first, a great source of encouragement, to Carolyn Banks, a fine critic, and to Carol Querolo Bartz, for checking on inscriptions. As always, I am indebted to my husband, Joe Osborn, for his continual interest and patience, and to Edward Simmen, who knew the island better than all of us.

Wings Press was founded in 1975 by Joanie Whitebird and Joseph Lomax, both deceased, as "an informal association of artists and cultural mythologists dedicated to the preservation of the literature of the nation of Texas." Publisher, editor and designer since 1995, Bryce Milligan is honored to carry on and expand that mission to include the finest in American writing—meaning all of the Americas—without commercial considerations clouding the choice to publish or not to publish.

Wings Press publishes multicultural books, chapbooks, CDs and DVDs that, we hope, enlighten the human spirit and enliven the mind. Every person ever associated with Wings has been or is a writer, and we know well that writing is a transformational art form capable of changing the world, primarily by allowing us to glimpse something of each other's souls. Good writing is innovative, insightful, and interesting. But most of all it is honest.

Likewise, Wings Press is committed to treating the planet itself as a partner. Thus the press uses as much recycled material as possible, from the paper on which the books are printed to the boxes in which they are shipped. All inks and papers used meet or exceed United States health and safety requirements.

As Robert Dana wrote in *Against the Grain,* "Small press publishing is personal publishing. In essence, it's a matter of personal vision, personal taste and courage, and personal friendships." Welcome to the Wings Press community of readers.

Colophon

This first edition of *Uncertain Ground*, by
Carolyn Osborn, has been printed on 55
pound Edwards Brothers Natural Paper con-
taining a high percentage of recycled fiber.
Titles have been set in Colonna type, the
text in Adobe Caslon type. All Wings Press
books are designed and produced by Bryce
Milligan.

On-line catalogue and ordering
available at
www.wingspress.com

Wings Press titles are distributed
to the trade by the
Independent Publishers Group
www.ipgbook.com

DISCARDED